Y0-AIP-011

At Issue

| Universal Health Care

Other Books in the At Issue Series

Athlete Activism
Celebrities in Politics
Male Privilege
Mob Rule or the Wisdom of the Crowd?
The Opioid Crisis
Public Outrage and Protest
Sexual Consent
Student Debt
Vaccination
Vaping
Wrongful Conviction and Exoneration

At Issue

Universal Health Care

Marcia Amidon Lusted, Book Editor

GREENHAVEN
PUBLISHING

Published in 2020 by Greenhaven Publishing, LLC
353 3rd Avenue, Suite 255, New York, NY 10010

Copyright © 2020 by Greenhaven Publishing, LLC

First Edition

All rights reserved. No part of this book may be reproduced in any form without permission in writing from the publisher, except by a reviewer.

Articles in Greenhaven Publishing anthologies are often edited for length to meet page requirements. In addition, original titles of these works are changed to clearly present the main thesis and to explicitly indicate the author's opinion. Every effort is made to ensure that Greenhaven Publishing accurately reflects the original intent of the authors. Every effort has been made to trace the owners of the copyrighted material.

Cover image: Lightspring/Shutterstock.com

Library of Congress Cataloging-in-Publication Data

Names: Lusted, Marcia Amidon, editor.
Title: Universal health care / Marcia Amidon Lusted, book editor.
Description: First edition. | New York : Greenhaven Publishing, 2020. | Series: At issue | Includes bibliographical references and index. | Audience: Grades 9–12.
Identifiers: LCCN 2019022816 | ISBN 9781534506268 (library binding) | ISBN 9781534506251 (paperback)
Subjects: LCSH: Health care reform—United States—Juvenile literature. | Medical care—United States—Juvenile literature.
Classification: LCC RA395.A3 U588 2020 | DDC 362.1/04250973—dc23
LC record available at https://lccn.loc.gov/2019022816

Manufactured in the United States of America

Website: http://greenhavenpublishing.com

Contents

Introduction   7

1. Health Is a Human Right, Right?   11
   Kisha Braithwaite
2. Understand How Insurance Works Before Debating Health Care Policy   18
   Gary M. Galles
3. Universal Health Care Should Be a Priority   22
   Ategeka Frank
4. The Politics of Universal Health Coverage   26
   Scott L. Greer and Claudio A. Méndez
5. Why Insurance Companies Control Your Medical Care   35
   Christy Ford Chapin
6. What Are Medicare and Medicaid?   42
   Nicole Galan
7. Medical Bankruptcy and the Economy   52
   Kimberly Amadeo
8. Is the ER Better Than Primary Care?   57
   Robert Wood Johnson Foundation
9. It's Inevitable, Single Payer Health Care Is Coming to America   61
   Ed Dolan
10. What Is "Single-Payer" Health Care?   68
    Meridian Paulton
11. Is Universal Health Care Still Unthinkable in America?   77
    Adam Gaffney
12. 7 Reasons Why Universal Health Care Won't Work in the US   83
    Kevin Mercadante
13. The Affordable Care Act: Past, Present, and Future   91
    Gilbert Berdine

14. Comparing US Health Costs to Other Countries *Aaron Hankin*	**100**
15. A Free-Market Solution to Health Care Reform *Kent Holtorf*	**105**
16. The Case for a Two-Tier Health System *Jonathan Gruber*	**110**

Organizations to Contact   **117**

Bibliography   **121**

Index   **125**

Introduction

On December 10, 1948, the United Nations proclaimed a Universal Declaration of Human Rights. For the first time, it set in writing exactly what fundamental human rights should be for all people in the world and that these rights must be universally protected.

The declaration covered many aspects of human life, including education, employment, and the treatment of women. It also stated that all human beings are born free and equal in dignity and rights. One article in particular addressed the issue of health and well-being. Article 25 of the declaration reads:

> *Everyone has the right to a standard of living adequate for the health and well-being of himself and of his family, including food, clothing, housing and medical care and necessary social services, and the right to security in the event of unemployment, sickness, disability, widowhood, old age or other lack of livelihood in circumstances beyond his control.*[1]

The United Nations and the World Health Organization also issued a fact sheet titled "The Right to Health," emphasizing the importance of health in just about every aspect of human life:

> *As human beings, our health and the health of those we care about is a matter of daily concern. Regardless of our age, gender, socio-economic or ethnic background, we consider our health to be our most basic and essential asset. Ill health, on the other hand, can keep us from going to school or to work, from attending to our family responsibilities or from participating fully in the activities of our community.*[2]

Clearly good health and access to health is seen as one of the basic rights of all people everywhere. But being able to access and pay for quality health care has become one of the major issues that modern individuals and families must wrestle with. In some countries, such as the United Kingdom and Canada, health care is provided to every citizen by the government, paid for through taxes. For example, Canadians receive their health care primarily from the province they live in, with some of it coming from the federal government. According to the Canadian government website, it is paid for "with general revenue raised through federal, provincial and territorial taxes, such as personal and corporate taxes, sales taxes, payroll levies and other revenue. Provinces may also charge a health premium on their residents to help pay for publicly funded health care services, but non-payment of a premium must not limit access to medically necessary health services."[3] In some countries, especially those that are not as developed, health care is difficult to access and is of uneven quality. Many people lack access to modern health care procedures and medicines and may not even have clean water and sufficient food to keep them healthy. According to the World Health Organization, half of the people in the world lack access to affordable health care, and for more than 100 million people, the cost of medical bills has driven their families into poverty.

In the United States, most people depend on health insurance to pay the costs of their medical care, both preventative and in the event of injury or illness. Some receive health insurance through their employers, usually at a cost that is deducted from their paychecks. Self-employed people, or those whose employers do not offer health insurance, may purchase private health insurance, although this is often extremely expensive. Elderly people, as well as those with limited resources, may receive health care under Medicare or Medicaid, two government-funded programs available to Americans who met the eligibility criteria to participate. Then there are people who cannot afford any form of health insurance, are not eligible because they do not work full-time, or risk going without insurance because they are young and healthy.

The United States has moved toward creating a system of health care that everyone in the country can use, regardless of their income or employment status. In 2010, the Affordable Care Act (nicknamed "Obamacare" because it was passed under President Barack Obama's administration) was passed, with the intention of providing affordable health care coverage to more people. This law included providing "consumers with subsidies ('premium tax credits') that lower costs for households with incomes between 100% and 400% of the federal poverty level."[4] It also sought to expand the Medicaid program to all adults living below 138% of the federal poverty level, and finally, to support new ways of delivering health care and lower the general costs of health care for everyone.[5]

However, since the election of President Donald Trump in 2016, the idea of a universal health care system for Americans has been an increasing source of conflict. Democrats are struggling to keep the Affordable Care Act in place, while President Trump has vowed to dismantle the program. And yet his administration has largely continued to enforce the ACA, even though it has shifted some of the responsibility for the law from the federal government to the states.

As the United States looks toward another presidential election, it is clear that the question of whether the country should have a system of universal health care comparable to that of other western countries like England and Canada will be debated and studied more frequently. *At Issue: Universal Health Care* offers a wide variety of viewpoints about universal health care and how effective it is, as well as whether it can work for the US the way it works for other countries, or if the US would have to create an entirely new version of universal health care in order to meet the needs and wants of both citizens and politicians. However, one thing seems clear: for many Americans, the costs of medical care, both for everyday ailments and procedures and for catastrophic injuries and illnesses, is fast becoming an impossible economic burden. Medical costs are soaring, and even insured families may find themselves driven into economic chaos by an unexpected hospitalization or a chronic illness. There are too many Americans who must choose between buying their medication and buying food. It remains to be seen if Americans and their politicians can agree on a better system than the one that is currently in place.

Notes

1. "Universal Declaration of Human Rights." United Nations, December 10, 1948. https://www.un.org/en/universal-declaration-human-rights.
2. "The Right to Health." United Nations Fact Sheet No. 31. 2008. https://www.ohchr.org/Documents/Publications/Factsheet31.pdf.
3. "Canada's Health Care System." Government of Canada, accessed April 28, 2019. https://www.canada.ca/en/health-canada/services/health-care-system/reports-publications/health-care-system/canada.html.
4. "Affordable Care Act (ACA)." Healthcare.gov, accessed April 28, 2019. https://www.healthcare.gov/glossary/affordable-care-act.
5. "Affordable Care Act (ACA)." Healthcare.gov.

1

Health Is a Human Right, Right?

Kisha Braithwaite

Dr. Kisha Braithwaite is a psychologist and associate professor in the Department of Psychiatry and Behavioral Sciences, Department of Community Health and Preventive Medicine, at the Morehouse School of Medicine in Atlanta, Georgia. She specializes in the fields of public health and mental/behavioral health.

In the following viewpoint, Dr. Kisha Braithwaite argues that while health care should be a basic human right for everyone, American society has often overlooked this right, resulting in millions of American citizens being uninsured, or being overwhelmed by the difficulty and expense of navigating through the US health care system. Health should not be a luxury. Public health affects us all. There cannot be healthy communities until the injustices of the health care system are addressed.

The constitution of the World Health Organization states that "the enjoyment of the highest attainable standard of health is one of the fundamental rights of every human being."[1](p1) Although this perspective is notable and has proven to be significant in promoting the quality of life among individuals worldwide, it is unfortunate that this resounding message is often not heard—and too often overlooked—by many parts of American society. Sadly, this basic human right is even more difficult to

"Health Is a Human Right, Right?" by Kisha Braithwaite, American Public Health Association, October 10, 2011. Reprinted by permission.

achieve for the estimated 43.3 million uninsured persons in the United States,[2] many of whom are poor, underserved, and underrepresented. Furthermore, the individuals who do have health insurance experience major difficulties navigating a fragmented health care system, accessing culturally responsive and quality health care, and securing associated finances.

Every day, working people struggle to make ends meet with health ailments that progressively worsen, in part because of their inability to comfortably connect with a health care provider and establish a medical "base." In some cases, the fear of receiving bad news about their health from a physician or the stigma associated with seeking mental health treatment may prevent individuals from expeditiously moving forward for health care. Yet, what may be even more daunting is the reality of the medical bills that will most certainly accompany any visit to a health care facility. Sociocultural, economic, political, and environmental tribulations continue to plague our communities and infect our health care systems, resulting in public health crises, disease epidemics, and enduring health disparities, placing vulnerable populations at increased risk of premature mortality and lives filled with suffering.

The distribution of health outcomes is extremely unbalanced across population groups in regard to race and gender.[3] African American men have the shortest life expectancy (69.2 years) among the four major race-gender groups in the United States (White women, 80.5 years; White men, 75.4 years; African American women, 76.1 years).[4] It is essential to understand that pervasive inequities have a detrimental impact on the physical and mental health status of many individuals, families, and communities. We must adopt the principle that health requires more than just health care. Needed attention to selected social determinants of health has been offered to the general public through provocative documentaries such as *Unnatural Causes … Is Inequality Making Us Sick?*[5] and *Sicko*.[6]

Nonetheless, much more remains to be done. In addition to honing in on micro-level connections between exposures and outcomes, there remains an enormous need to examine, at a macro level, the interrelated research, practice, and policy issues that are important for societies that seek to achieve social justice for all and health as a human right.

Social Policy Is Health Policy

Traditional presumptions rooted in the medical model about the causes of diseases and disabilities have hindered multidimensional explanations about determinants of health problems because of overrepresentation of the concepts of individual physiopathological development and familial predisposition. Although these are important considerations and powerful ideologies, they limit critical thinking about additional means for confronting health inequities. A discourse based on social justice supports the notion of a multi-dimensional collective schema for achieving healthy communities while also addressing the social and economic conditions that are at the core of health inequities and health disparities.

The creation of healthy communities depends upon the realization and organization of the vital conditions of everyday life. These conditions include such things as the quality and affordability of housing, level of employment and job security, standard of living, income level, availability and quality of mass transportation, education, social services, crime rates, air and water quality, economic development, racism, sexism, poverty, workplace conditions, and political equality.[7] As such, social policy is intertwined with health policy, because they both have similar emerging issues that have consequences for achieving equity and related systemic barriers that may slow progress. Thus, when policy solutions are achieved for one ideology, they can have bidirectional and synergistic effects.

It is imperative that the development of strategies that promote health equity simultaneously address social, economic, and civil inequalities. Eliminating health inequities is a theme of social justice, because health is central to individual productivity and the creation of communities that can thrive. We must continue to make strides that promote urgency in methods for achieving collective actions with systematic, institutional, and political legitimacy, despite conventional public expectations that currently reinforce boundaries.

Toward Health Justice

US expenditures on health care exceed those of any other nation, yet the people of the United States experience some of the poorest health outcomes in the industrialized world.[8] Health and health care considerations rank among the top priorities for Americans who plan to vote in the November 2008 presidential election. Thus, policymakers should determine the best strategies to address the myriad concerns that contribute to failing health and poor health outcomes, as well as carefully scrutinize the options that will ultimately impact millions of individuals.

The Democratic candidate, Senator Barack Obama, has stated that

> *We now face an opportunity—and an obligation—to turn the page on the failed politics of yesterday's health care debates.... My plan begins by covering every American.*[9]

According to the Republican candidate, Senator John McCain,

> *The goal, after all, is to make the best care available to everyone. We want a system of health care in which everyone can afford and acquire the treatment and preventative care they need, and the peace of mind that comes with knowing they are covered. Health care in America should be affordable by all, not just the wealthy.*[10]

If these statements are to live up to their promise, the next US president—whomever that might be—must take a very deliberate approach to restructuring our current system of health care.

It is our responsibility, as public health researchers, clinicians, and policy- and decisionmakers, to become involved in the progression of innovative methods and acts of service that reinforce systematic health care transformation. Accordingly, this legacy issue of the *Journal* represents a collection of thought-provoking work by some of the most respected intellectuals who are dedicated to improving public health and building healthy communities. Historical, contextual, relevant, and meaningful frameworks about health from multidisciplinary perspectives are presented in a comprehensive manner.

Highlights include an examination of the role that race and racism play in influencing the deleterious individual, institutional, and situational health consequences on health disparities for ethnically, culturally, and racially diverse populations. Health care systems are also explored, and evidence is amassed to build and support the case for health care reform, expansion of health insurance coverage, greater attention on addressing the health care concerns of vulnerable groups, increased access to comprehensive care, and development of health policies to improve the health and health care of disenfranchised individuals and families as a part of a larger social movement for health justice.

A closer look at oral health, a neglected epidemic, is presented. Credence is provided to the burden of oral diseases and influences on social and economic factors for impoverished urban and rural communities. The incidence and prevalence of mental illnesses, substance abuse, and psychosocial and behavioral health problems experienced by children, youth, and adults demand due attention and resources.

Questions about appropriate assessment, diagnoses, and access to viable treatments remain unanswered, despite being repeatedly raised. The delivery of health care services may be further complicated by the disjointed systems that are currently available. Prevention and intervention approaches, research priorities, and advocacy efforts toward improving mental health outcomes and promoting overall health and well-being within families, communities, and societies are discussed.

The historical and complex reasons for men's poor health outcomes are disentangled and analyzed, and the unique stressors encountered by African American men are illuminated. Social structural discord, exclusionary health policies, poverty, race, and unhealthy behaviors are identified as some of the quandaries that have catapulted the rates of chronic disease and premature death for men of color to the top of the list. Finally, the interface between the criminal justice system and the health care system is inspected. Approximately 650,000 ex-offenders are released annually. Needs of those seeking community reentry and needs of communities absorbing ex-offenders go unmet. Furthermore, there are currently close to 2.2 million men and women who are housed in prisons and jails in the United States,[11] and a growing body of evidence points to levels of ill health before, during, and after incarceration, including high rates of infectious diseases, such as HIV/AIDS.

The two main goals of *Healthy People* 2010[12] are clear: namely, to (1) help individuals of all ages increase life expectancy and improve their quality of life and (2) eliminate health disparities among different segments of the population. To have any hope of achieving these targets, we must seek health justice for all. To the question, "Health is a human right, right?" the collective community voice must be an emphatic "Yes!"

Notes

1. World Health Organization. Constitution of the World Health Organization. Available at: http://www.who.int/governance/eb/who_constitution_en.pdf. Accessed June 15, 2008.
2. Centers for Disease Control and Prevention. Health insurance coverage. Available at: http://www.cdc.gov/nchs/fastats/hinsure.htm. Accessed June 15, 2008.
3. House JS, Williams DR. Understanding and reducing socioeconomic racial/ethnic disparities in health. In: Hofrichter R, ed. *Health and Social Justice: Politics, Ideology, and Inequity in the Distribution of Disease*. San Francisco, CA: Jossey-Bass; 2003:89–131.
4. Centers for Disease Control and Prevention. Table 27. Life expectancy at birth, at 65 years of age, and at 75 years of age, by race and sex: United States, selected years 1900–2005. Available at: http://www.cdc.gov/nchs/data/hus/hus07.pdf#027. Accessed June 15, 2008.
5. *Unnatural Causes ... Is Inequality Making Us Sick?* [film]. Available at: http://www.unnaturalcauses.org. Accessed June 15, 2008.
6. Moore M. *Sicko*. [film]. Available at: http://www.michaelmoore.com/sicko/index.html. Accessed June 15, 2008.
7. Hofrichter, R. The politics of health inequities: contested terrain. In: Hofrichter R, ed. *Health and Social Justice: Politics, Ideology, and Inequity in the Distribution of Disease*. San Francisco, CA: Jossey-Bass; 2003:1–56.

8. Boat TF, Chao SM, O'Neill PH. From waste to value in health care. *JAMA*. 2008;299:568–571. Crossref, Medline.
9. Quote from Senator Barack Obama, Speech in Iowa City, Iowa, May 29, 2007. Available at: http://www.barackobama.com. Accessed June 15, 2008.
10. Quote from Senator John McCain, Speech in Tampa, Fla, April 29, 2008. Available at: http://www.johnmccain.com. Accessed June 15, 2008.
11. US Department of Justice. Prison statistics. Washington, DC: Office of Justice Programs, Bureau of Justice Statistics; June 2007. Available at: http://www.ojp.usdoj.gov/bjs/prisons.htm. Accessed June 15, 2008.
12. World Health Organization. *Healthy People 2010: Understanding and Improving Health*. Available at: http://www.healthypeople.gov. Accessed June 15, 2008.

2

Understand How Insurance Works Before Debating Health Care Policy

Gary M. Galles

Gary M. Galles is a professor of economics at Pepperdine University. His recent books include Faulty Premises, Faulty Policies *(2014) and* Apostle of Peace *(2013). He is a member of the FEE Faculty Network.*

Most Americans fail to fully understand how health insurance works. Insurance is about risk, not about price controls or mandated coverage, argues Gary Galles. The government does not help educate policy-holders either and, according to the author, is instead misinforming them with miscalculations and overpromising.

For at least half a century (Medicare turned 50 last year), health insurance policies have been hotly debated. The most recent skirmish is over the Trump administration's final rule expanding the availability of short-term, limited-coverage insurance. Single-payer and Obamacare stalwarts have attacked it tooth and nail. For instance, *Los Angeles Times* columnist David Lazarus asserted backers "have no clue how insurance works" because they "decided to skip class when the topic of insurance came up in Econ 101."

Unfortunately, if accurately applying principles of insurance is the standard, both single-payer and Obamacare fans compare

---

"Understand How Insurance Works Before Debating Health Care Policy," by Gary M. Galles, Foundation for Economic Education, August 7, 2018. https://fee.org/articles/understand-how-insurance-works-before-debating-health-care-policy/. Licensed under CC BY 4.0 International.

poorly to pots calling kettles black. Their preferred policies sharply conflict with insurance principles on multiple fronts.

Insurance Is All About Risk and the Unknown

Insurance is about reducing risk from uncertain events. It makes outcomes for a group with similar risks more predictable. But that must be weighed against the additional administrative and other costs of insurance. That would mean that people would not insure against what would happen for certain nor where there is only a small amount of risk reduction provided if they were spending their own money.

Insuring things which would occur with certainty, say certain inoculations and annual checkups, offers no risk reduction. It provides no added benefits to weigh against the added costs of insurance administration, yet government plans mandate such coverage. Similarly, small health care risks are cheaper to cover directly out of modest savings than incurring the added costs of insurance administration, but government plans also mandate such coverage. Few would want such coverage unless much of the cost was forced onto others (which is how Obamacare subsidies muted criticism of such inefficiencies).

Further, any benefits from reducing risk would also have to exceed added costs induced by insurance coverage. When insurance covers most of the costs, it makes care artificially cheap to recipients, just like a subsidy (e.g., if a medical treatment cost $1,000, someone who had 80 percent coverage would face a cost of only $200). Those artificially low costs to recipients increase the quantity and quality of care they desire. That will increase medical utilization and costs (called moral hazard in the insurance literature), much of which would not be worth the real cost (e.g., above, someone who valued a $1,000 service at $250, but had 80 percent coverage, would still want it, even though it wastes $750 in value). And the ensuring waste can be very large because there are many margins at which those insured will want better care (e.g., better and more specialized doctors and hospitals, more costly newer drugs, tests, and treatment, etc.) as well as more care, raising costs (or requiring care to be rationed, making treatment unavailable, even with insurance, to those on the losing end of such allocation).

Further, differences in circumstances and preferences mean that not everyone would want the same coverage. Teetotalers confident of remaining so would not willingly insure for alcoholism treatment. Those sure they would never use drugs would not want to bear the cost of providing addiction treatment. Yet government mandates that many such medical services be covered, reflecting the political power of provider lobbying far more than the values recipients place on them.

Insurance Is Not About Price Controls or Mandated Coverage

The price controls government health care proposals incorporate also violate insurance principles. For instance, my age makes my actuarial risk roughly six times that of my students. Pooling risks among those similarly situated with me can benefit us; pooling risks among those similarly situated with my students can benefit them. Insurance is based on pooling risks among people whose risks are comparable. But incorporating more people with risk differentials (say, 6 to 1) that are different from their premium differentials (say, 3 to 1) forces the overpriced people to subsidize the underpriced people. That is not motivated by insurance principles. It is wealth redistribution.

It is redistribution, not insurance, which motivates that, and explains why Obamacare imposed penalties to force the losers to accept a bad deal.

Mandating coverage of pre-existing conditions, always emphasized by fans of government health plans, is also revealing. Such a mandate doesn't reduce everyone's risk exposure, it just forces someone else to cover certain people's already-known-to-be-higher costs while allowing blame to be deflected onto insurance companies who must charge other policyholders more. And it is worth remembering that casinos don't let you bet after the roulette ball or dice have stopped moving, nor are they offered in fire, automobile, or life insurance.

Equally instructive is the treatment of catastrophic coverage—the type of coverage most consistent with insurance principles—under Obamacare. It allows the most valuable risk reduction—from very costly, uncertain events—while limiting the overconsumption of medical care. But Obamacare was so slanted against them that less than 1 percent of policyholders chose the option most consistent with insurance principles. In particular, catastrophic coverage was restricted to people under 30, unless one could get a special exemption (and especially with guaranteed subsidized family coverage extended to 26-year-olds, that is a small group), and the subsidies available to those in the "metallic" plans were not available to catastrophic plans.

Politics Ruins the Purpose of Insurance

There is also the fact that insurance principles are based on actual probabilities. They do not justify lies and misrepresentations. But Obamacare was supported with a host of them, from, "you can keep your own doctor" to known-to-be-false claims of bending down the medical cost curve and providing $2,600 annual savings per family. Insurance companies would not even survive such fraudulent claims. Similarly, single-payer or Medicare for all plans use estimates of costs off by trillions of dollars and preposterous assertions of how they could be funded. Such misrepresentation cannot be part of insurance policies that will advance Americans' well-being.

One would think that government health plan backers might be more circumspect in their assertions of opponents' cluelessness about insurance principles because the plans they support trample insurance principles beyond recognition. But then, how often do government claims of adhering to principles increase the likelihood that those claims are true?

3

Universal Health Care Should Be a Priority
Ategeka Frank

Ategeka Frank was born to Rwandan refugees in Uganda in 1988. He is a 2018–2019 Global Health Corps (GHC) fellow at the Center for Health, Human Rights & Development in Uganda and the cofounder and team leader of Rural Aid Foundation Uganda.

On a worldwide scale, at least half of the world's population lacks access to basic health services, and millions more are pushed into poverty by their health care expenses. Refugees are especially vulnerable, and there is a health care crisis in countries that find themselves hosting large numbers of refugees. It will require strong partnerships at the community, national, regional, and global levels to address the critical need for health care services.

Universal health coverage (UHC) means that all people and communities receive the quality health services they need without suffering financial hardship. To reach this goal, the international community now recognizes Universal Health Coverage (UHC) Day on December 12, since the adoption of a resolution by the United Nations (UN) General Assembly in Tokyo in December 2017. At the same time, the UN adopted another resolution establishing UHC2030, a health system platform that promotes multi-stakeholder collaboration to advance global efforts towards achieving UHC by the year 2030.

"Prioritize Refugee Health Needs for Universal Health Coverage by 2030," by Ategeka Frank, Medium.com, January 19, 2019. Reprinted by permission.

Impact of Health Inequities on Vulnerable Communities

The publication of new data in the Tracking Universal Health Coverage: 2017 Global Monitoring Report revealed that at least half of the world's population still lack access to essential health services and about 100 million people are pushed into extreme poverty each year because of their health expenditures. According to the report, although they may have access to some health services, more than half of the world's 7.3 billion people do not receive all of the essential health services they need. Essential health services encompass everything from health promotion to prevention, treatment, rehabilitation, and palliative care throughout the course of a lifetime. These include neonatal, child, adolescent and maternal health, sexual and reproductive health, infectious diseases, non-communicable diseases, and more.

Additionally, over 800 million people spend at least 10 percent of their household budgets to pay for health care. What does this mean to a poor person in a rural community living below the global poverty line ($1.90 per day)? It means if one's household annual budget is $1000, they spend at least $100 on health care. With this, one may not explicitly understand the adverse effects of huge health expenditures on one's life. Now consider an unemployed person. The annual household income is usually very small to cover all their expenditures. What does this mean when it comes to paying for health services? It means that a person will spend more than they earn on healthcare services and thus resort to borrowing and potentially being pushed into extreme poverty.

To exacerbate the situation, such challenges fall hardest on vulnerable persons like refugees who leave all their businesses, income generating activities, and investments in their home countries. This makes it challenging for them to access healthcare, and in many cases whether refugees live or die is determined by who and where they are.

Refugees Influx in Uganda: Health Equity Crisis

With Uganda currently hosting over one million refugees from several unstable African countries, there is a need for stakeholder engagement for increased support for refugee health needs to achieve UHC by 2030. As part of the global effort to support refugees, Uganda hosted Solidarity Summit on refugees on June 21 and 22, 2017, and the world gathered in Uganda to stand in solidarity with the country as we hosted over one million refugees. The summit, hosted by the honorable President of Uganda Yoweri Museveni and the United Nations Secretary-General Mr. Antonio Guterres, raised over USD 350 million to support the refugee crisis and influx in Uganda. Of course, health services support for the refugees was among the many social aspects that could be addressed by this commitment. The summit was a great multi-stakeholder engagement towards supporting refugees globally

Uganda's integrated refugee response incorporating host communities has been named as the model for the Comprehensive Refugee Response Framework (CRRF), adopted at the September 2016 UN Summit for Refugees and Migrants in New York. This makes Uganda a front line state for this new approach. Along with the UN High Commissioner for Refugees, the government of Uganda and other humanitarian agencies have done a great job addressing the health needs of the persons of concern. However there is still a need to build more partnerships between private, national, regional and global agencies towards supporting refugee health needs as we strive to achieve UHC by 2030. This means that more partners across sectors need to invest in supporting refugee health needs through increasing community awareness of UHC and calling for stakeholder cooperation to support refugee health needs.

Partnerships Are Key for Improved Refugee Health

The 2018 theme for UHC Day was "Unite for Universal Health Coverage: Now is the time for collective action." In Uganda, Rural Aid Foundation through Global Health Strategies was funded by

UHC2030 to commemorate UHC Day and engage the refugee community and different stakeholders in a dialogue on UHC. The event was also held in partnership with Global Health Corps young leaders including Caroline Achola from Days For Girls and Dennis Ernest Ssesanga and Hana Hamdi from IntraHealth Uganda. Other partners included InterAid Uganda, the Ministry of Health, Public Health Ambassadors, and Rise up for Refugees. Over 250 refugees and stakeholders attended, creating strong momentum for advancing the global UHC 2030 strategy in Uganda with a specific focus on refugee health rights and government commitments and policies to protect and uphold those rights.

After the dialogue, various stakeholders committed to supporting refugee health needs and driving the UHC 2030 agenda by engaging other stakeholders at national, regional and global levels. They made a call to government and other stakeholders to prioritize refugee health needs for UHC.

Universal Health Coverage, SDGs, and UHC Advocacy Principles

As endorsed in the UHC2030 Global Compact, two key principles were broadly fulfilled, including:

- Leaving no one behind: a commitment to equity, non-discrimination, and a human rights-based approach
- Making health systems everybody's business: engaging citizens, communities, civil society, and the private sector in achieving UHC

Expanding access to affordable, quality healthcare to refugees will require continued partnership at the community, national, regional, and global levels. To achieve UHC globally, states must prioritize and address the health challenges for the most vulnerable populations, including refugees, to ensure no one is left behind.

4

The Politics of Universal Health Coverage

Scott L. Greer and Claudio A. Méndez

Scott L. Greer is with the University of Michigan School of Public Health, Ann Arbor. Claudio A. Méndez is with the Instituto de Salud Pública, Universidad Austral de Chile, Valdivia.

In public health policy, universal health care has become a major point of discussion. But it is often presented as a technical project that should be carried out cooperatively by communities and the medical establishment. However, the authors of this article argue that there are studies and literature that point to the absolute necessity for government and political policy involvement in establishing universal health care.

Universal health coverage has become a rallying cry in health policy, but it is often presented as a consensual, technical project. It is not.

A review of the broader international literature on the origins of universal coverage shows that it is intrinsically political and cannot be achieved without recognition of its dependence on, and consequences for, both governance and politics.

On one hand, a variety of comparative research has shown that health coverage is associated with democratic political accountability. Democratization, and in particular left-wing parties, gives governments particular cause to expand health

"Universal Health Coverage: A Political Struggle and Governance Challenge," by Scott L. Greer and Claudio A. Méndez, American Public Health Association, October 28, 2015. Reprinted by permission.

coverage. On the other hand, governance, the ways states make and implement decisions, shapes any decision to strive for universal health coverage and the shape of its implementation.

Universal health coverage (UHC) has become a focal point in global health conversations. In the spirit of previous unifying concepts such as Health for All, basic health needs, and the Alma-Ata declaration, it presents a vision in which all citizens will enjoy (1) a strong and efficient health system that spans preventive and curative medicine, (2) affordable access to that health system, (3) access to relevant medicines, and (4) sufficient human resources for the health system. The 2010 World Health Report presented UHC as an objective and a strategy for its member states to reform, or design, their health systems.[1] UHC has been the focus of much research and policy prescription since then. Various authors have shown its implications for the health workforce and its governance,[2,3] health financing,[4] and management.[5]

But is UHC likely to be attained? We draw on political science and public health literature to argue that politics and governance have been undervalued as key drivers for universal health coverage.

Universal Health Coverage Is Political

It is a political victory that UHC is discussed at all, and still more so that it has any veneer of consensus. UHC is a highly political concept. In the world of global health governance, it is part of an ongoing debate about the relative importance of "vertical" priorities such as disease eradication and broader "horizontal" system-strengthening proposals.[6,7] Given the momentum behind disease-specific interventions and the appeal of solving particular problems (e.g., antiretrovirals or polio eradication), it is always difficult to argue for more amorphous health system goals that are part of UHC or predecessor agendas.[8]

The contentiousness of global health politics is nothing like the domestic politics of UHC or universal health care access by any other name. The US State Department has even objected to a World Health Organization fact sheet on the right to health.[9] Observation of politics in the United States,[10, 11] or reading about the history of health politics anywhere, supports this point. UHC is expensive and redistributive; that is enough to make it contentious.[12, 13] As if that were not enough, UHC also builds in additional contentious goals such as efficiency or access and medicines.[14–16] It is unwise to assume that UHC goals are entrenched in the countries that have broadly achieved them, to overstate the influence of health ministries or advocates committed to UHC, or to overstate the degree of consensus among governments that have adopted them on paper.[17, 18]

If any generalization about UHC holds, it is that democratization promotes it. Middle-income countries can broadly afford to aim for UHC, but they are most likely to enact access expansions when they have governments that are accountable to the population.[19–21] The effects of widespread democratization from the 1970s to the late 1990s help to explain the expansion of UHC in middle-income countries today.[22–25] Authoritarian regimes, by contrast, are less responsive to the broad population, can discourage or repress organized challenges, and therefore often focus benefits on a narrower set of people who are part of the regime or who can threaten it (e.g., by striking or staging a military coup). The result has been the historical pattern of segmentation that southern Europe and Latin America have had to confront, in which a few crucial sets of workers (especially the public sector and key strategic industries) enjoy extensive health and other benefits and groups without the capacity to threaten the regime receive less.[19, 26–28]

Partisan politics are one of the most promising avenues for explaining UHC. In particular, left-wing parties are more likely to enact redistributive policies such as UHC.[27, 29–31] Socialist parties enacted universal health care across southern Europe when they came to power after democratization,[32] despite major recessions that might be expected to block health access expansion, and later it was the left that universalized health care in Latin American countries such as Brazil and Chile.[33, 34] Conservative parties have also at times expanded health coverage for their own political purposes.[20, 35] Otto von Bismarck created the first social health insurance in response to socialist challenges, Japan's health insurance expansion came about as a response to a left labor challenge to the dominant conservative Liberal Democratic Party, and the expansion of health care access in Mexico was partly a strategy to maintain the popularity of its once-dominant Party of the Institutional Revolution.[36, 37]

Democracy and partisanship do not automatically produce UHC; UHC still needs organized support and faces organized opposition.[38–40] Unorganized voters are unlikely to have their preferences reflected in any political system. The complexities of organization, political coalitions, and parties, a long-standing issue in comparative politics, therefore demand attention; the relationship between left-party success and UHC policies is not simple,[31] and part of the reason is the interaction between politics and governance.

Governance

"Good governance" is a widely supported goal, but there is great disagreement about what it is and how it is to be attained.[41, 42] Governance discussion often mixes governance as a phenomenon (how decisions are made) with normative policy advice (how decisions should be made and implemented, i.e., good governance). Governance as a phenomenon is the institutional framework of the decisions and policy implementation.[43] A review of components of governance in the health and broader policy literatures by authors associated with the European Observatory on Health Systems and Policies found that diverse authors focused on the same five areas in which governance can affect health systems: transparency, participation, accountability, integrity (management and anticorruption measures), and policymaking capacity.[44]

Governance shapes the likelihood that UHC will be adopted and actually implemented for three reasons. First, it is a prerequisite for some policies. Just as policies for UHC can cost too much for a given state, they can also demand a level of expertise, accountability, and good public administration that is not always available. In particular, elaborate public-private, market-based, and personal insurance schemes can overwhelm the capacity to design, regulate, and operate them.[44]

Second, governance, particularly political institutions, can shape the likelihood of pro-UHC forces winning in politics. Veto points at which a policy can be blocked include bicameralism, referenda, strong supreme courts, and some forms of federalism; they are correlated with slower increases of expenditure, less redistribution, and less programmatic coherence, although they also slow retrenchment.[29] Among the rich countries, the United States and Switzerland stand out for the expense, slow development, and inegalitarianism of their health systems and for their particularly high number of veto points. Their many veto points make opposition easier, demand larger political coalitions, and allow interest groups to extract a higher price for their support.[45-48]

Third, governance affects the likelihood that programs will be entrenched by affording programs greater or lesser real effectiveness and greater or lesser political defenses. Although the post-Communist states have shown that it is politically very difficult to take away UHC,[19] their experiences also show that a system that only formally delivers UHC can engender effective privatization through exit from the system (into private provision) or informal payments. Ineffective programs engender less loyalty. Alternatively, governments can lock in UHC achievements by making the systems transparent and accountable to affected groups who will in the future be able to ward off efforts to reduce government commitments or undermine achievements.[49] A well-crafted policy includes governance changes that promote its own political survival by biasing policymaking toward groups who defend UHC. Just as Latin American's military regimes left institutional safeguards for their interests,[50] UHC advocates should pay attention to ways they can create institutional safeguards for a right to health. "Policies create politics," after all.[51]

Conclusions

There is a strong tendency to discuss UHC as though it were a settled goal that only requires technical follow-up. This approach contradicts or at least underplays a large body of evidence suggesting that UHC is potentially transformative and intensely political, and depends on the features of a country's governance. Without support in domestic politics, a redistributive policy such as UHC is unlikely to happen. Without political support in the international arena, it can be undermined by advocates of other attractive goals such as programs focused on single diseases. Decision-making and implementation—governance—can support or hinder UHC advocates and deserve attention for the ways in which they can bias decisions and improve or hinder implementation.

For researchers, this means that we need to apply ourselves to better understanding the mechanisms connecting governance, political forces, and UHC decisions; although studies have pointed to the interplay of parties and institutions under democratization, much still remains to be understood about the coalitions and political strategies that shape UHC politics. For UHC advocates, this means that technical skills and advice should be regarded as resources to be used in what are ultimately political fights within countries, that the commitment to UHC by member states is a resource for political argument rather than a binding obligation, and that attention to health governance should come with an explicit objective of strengthening those who seek UHC.

Notes

1. World Health Organization. Health Systems Financing: The Path to Universal Health Coverage. Geneva, Switzerland: World Health Organization; 2010.
2. Koon AD, Mayhew SH. Strengthening the health workforce and rolling out universal health coverage: the need for policy analysis. Glob Health Action. 2013;6:21852.

3. Sousa A, Scheffler RM, Nyoni J, Boerma T. A comprehensive health labour market framework for universal health coverage. Bull World Health Organ. 2013;91(11):892–894.
4. Kutzin J. Health financing for universal coverage and health system performance: concepts and implications for policy. Bull World Health Organ. 2013;91(8):602–611.
5. Fattore G, Tediosi F. The importance of values in shaping how health systems governance and management can support universal health coverage. Value Health. 2013;16(1 suppl):S19–S23.
6. Mills A. Mass campaigns versus general health services: what have we learnt in 40 years about vertical versus horizontal approaches? Bull World Health Organ. 2005;83(4):315–316.
7. Oliveira-Cruz V, Kurowski C, Mills A. Delivery of priority health services: searching for synergies within the vertical versus horizontal debate. *J Int Dev.* 2003;15(1):67–86.
8. Stepan NL. *Eradication: Ridding the World of Diseases Forever?* Ithaca, NY: Cornell University Press; 2011.
9. Berman ML. Pursuing global health with justice. *J Law Biosci.* 2014;1(3):348–358.
10. McDonough JE. *Inside National Health Reform*. Berkeley, CA: University of California Press; 2011.
11. Rice T, Unruh LY, Rosenau P, Barnes AJ, Saltman RB, van Ginneken E. Challenges facing the United States of America in implementing universal coverage. Bull World Health Organ. 2014;92(12):894–902.
12. O'Connell T, Rasanathan K, Chopra M. What does universal health coverage mean? *Lancet.* 2014;383(9913):277–279.
13. Evans RG. Financing health care: taxation and the alternatives. In: Mossialos E, Dixon A, Figueras J, Kutzin J, eds. *Funding Health Care: Options for Europe*. Buckingham, UK: Open University Press; 2002:31–58.
14. Roffe P, Tansey G, Vivas-Eugui D, eds. *Negotiating Health: Intellectual Property and Access to Medicines*. London, UK: Earthscan; 2006.
15. Sell SK. *Private Power, Public Law: The Globalization of Intellectual Property Rights*. New York, NY: Cambridge University Press; 2003.
16. Massard E. Intellectual property enforcement in the European Union. In: Greer SL, Kurzer P, eds. *European Union Public Health Policies: Regional and Global Perspectives*. Abingdon, UK: Routledge; 2013:126–138.
17. McKee M, Balabanova D, Basu S, Ricciardi W, Stuckler D. Universal health coverage: a quest for all countries but under threat in some. Value Health. 2013;16(1 suppl):S39–S45.
18. Borgonovi E, Compagni A. Sustaining universal health coverage: the interaction of social, political, and economic sustainability. Value Health. 2013;16(1 suppl):S34–S38.
19. Haggard S, Kaufman RR. *Development, Democracy, and Welfare States: Latin America, East Asia, and Eastern Europe*. Princeton, NJ: Princeton University Press; 2008.
20. Wong J. *Healthy Democracies: Welfare Politics in Taiwan and South Korea*. Ithaca, NY: Cornell University Press; 2004.
21. McGuire JW. *Wealth, Health, and Democracy in East Asia and Latin America*. Cambridge, UK: Cambridge University Press; 2010.
22. Lagomarsino G, Garabrant A, Adyas A, Muga R, Otoo N. Moving towards universal health coverage: health insurance reforms in nine developing countries in Africa and Asia. *Lancet.* 2012;380(9845):933–943.

23. Hicken A, Selway JS. Forcing the genie back in the bottle: sociological change, institutional reform, and health policy in Thailand. *J East Asian Stud*. 2012;12(1):57–88.
24. Aspinall E. Health care and democratization in Indonesia. Democratization. 2014;21(5):803–823.
25. Carbone G. Do new democracies deliver social welfare? Political regimes and health policy in Ghana and Cameroon. Democratization. 2012;19(2):157–183.
26. Cotlear D, Gomez-Dantes O, Knaul F, et al. Overcoming social segregation in health care in Latin America. *Lancet*. 2015;385(9974):1248–1259.
27. Teichman J. *Social Forces and States: Poverty and Distributional Outcomes in South Korea, Chile, and Mexico*. Redwood City, CA: Stanford University Press; 2012.
28. Toth F. Is there a southern European healthcare model? West Eur Polit. 2010;33(2):325–343.
29. Huber E, Stephens JD. *Development and Crisis of the Welfare State: Parties and Policies in Global Markets*. Chicago, IL: University of Chicago Press; 2001.
30. Huber E, Stephens JD. *Democracy and the Left: Social Policy and Inequality in Latin America*. Chicago, IL: University of Chicago Press; 2012.
31. Imbeau LM, Pétry F, Lamari M. Left-right party ideology and government policies: a meta-analysis. *Eur J Polit Res*. 2001;40(1):1–29.
32. Linos K. *The Democratic Foundations of Policy Diffusion: How Health, Family and Employment Laws Spread Across Countries*. New York, NY: Oxford University Press; 2013.
33. Mesa-Lago C. Social protection in Chile: reforms to improve equity. Int Labour Rev. 2008;147(4):377–402.
34. Bustamante AV, Méndez CA. Health care privatization in Latin America: comparing diverging privatization approaches in Chile, Colombia, and Mexico. *J Health Polit Policy Law*. 2014;39(4):841–886.
35. Ward PM. Social welfare policy and political opening in Mexico. *J Lat Am Stud*. 1993;25(3):613–628.
36. Campbell JC, Ikegami N. *The Art of Balance in Health Policy: Maintaining Japan's Low-Cost, Egalitarian System*. New York, NY: Cambridge University Press; 1998.
37. Homedes N, Ugalde A. Twenty-five years of convoluted health reforms in Mexico. PLoS Med. 2009;6(8):e1000124.
38. Kosack S. *The Education of Nations: How the Political Organization of the Poor, Not Democracy, Led Governments to Invest in Mass Education*. New York, NY: Oxford University Press; 2012.
39. Savedoff WD, de Ferranti D, Smith AL, Fan V. Political and economic aspects of the transition to universal health coverage. *Lancet*. 2012;380(9845):924–932.
40. Méndez CA. Global health politics: neither solidarity nor policy: Comment on "Globalization and the diffusion of ideas: why we should acknowledge the roots of mainstream ideas in global health." Int J Health Policy Manag 2014;3(2):103–105.
41. Grindle MS. Good enough governance: poverty reduction and reform in developing countries. Governance (Oxf). 2004;17(4):525–548.
42. Barbazza E, Tello JE. A review of health governance: definitions, dimensions and tools to govern. Health Policy. 2014;116(1):1–11.
43. World Bank. Governance and Development. Washington, DC: World Bank; 1992.
44. Greer SL, Wismar M, Figueras J, eds. *Strengthening Health System Governance: Better Policies, Stronger Performance*. Brussels, Belgium: European Observatory on Health Systems and Policies/Open University Press; 2015.

45. Immergut EM. *Health Politics: Interests and Institutions in Western Europe.* New York, NY: Cambridge University Press; 1992.
46. Quadagno J. *One Nation, Uninsured: Why the US Has No National Health Insurance.* New York, NY: Oxford University Press; 2005.
47. Ehrlich SD. *Access Points: An Institutional Theory of Policy Bias and Policy Complexity.* New York, NY: Oxford University Press; 2011.
48. Stepan A, Linz JJ. Comparative perspectives on inequality and the quality of democracy in the United States. Perspect Polit. 2011;9(4):841–856.
49. Greer SL, Lillvis DF. Beyond leadership: political strategies for coordination in health policies. Health Policy. 2014;116(1):12–17.
50. Ewig C, Kay SJ. Postretrenchment politics: policy feedback in Chile's health and pension reforms. Lat Am Polit Soc. 2011;53(4):67–99.
51. Schattschneider EE. *Politics, Pressures, and the Tariff.* New York, NY: Prentice Hall; 1935.

5

Why Insurance Companies Control Your Medical Care

Christy Ford Chapin

Christy Ford Chapin is an assistant professor in the history department at the University of Maryland Baltimore County (UMBC) and a visiting scholar at Johns Hopkins University. Her interests include political, business, and economic history, as well as capitalism studies. Her book, Ensuring America's Health: The Public Creation of the Corporate Health Insurance System, *was recently published by Cambridge University Press.*

Americans recognized they were living under a flawed health care system long before the Affordable Care Act was passed. As rates for insurance and prescriptions continue to skyrocket, Americans may wonder how we got to this place. There was a time before insurance, when doctors acted as their own insurers. Ironically, insurance companies were started because of concerns that doctor groups would turn into corporations. Of course, over time the result has been even worse—with insurance companies holding increasing power over medical professionals. We know the system is broken, but fixing it might prove impossible.

"Why Insurance Companies Control Your Medical Care," by Christy Ford Chapin, The Conversation, October 4, 2016. https://theconversation.com/why-insurance-companies-control-your-medical-care-62540. Licensed under CC BY ND 4.0 International.

Universal Health Care

It's that time of year again. Insurance companies that participate in the Affordable Care Act's state health exchanges are signaling that prices will rise dramatically this fall.

And if insurance costs aren't enough of a crisis, researchers are highlighting deficiencies in health care quality, such as unnecessary tests and procedures that cause patient harm, medical errors bred by disjointed or fragmented care and disparities in service distribution.

While critics emphasize the ACA's shortcomings, cost and quality issues have long plagued the US health care system. As my research demonstrates, we have these problems because insurance companies are at the center of the system, where they both finance and manage medical care.

If this system is so flawed, how did we get stuck with it in the first place?

Answer: organized physicians.

As I explain in my book, "Ensuring America's Health: The Public Creation of the Corporate Health Care System," from the 1930s through the 1960s, the American Medical Association, the foremost professional organization for physicians, played a leading role in implementing the insurance company model.

What Existed Before Health Insurance Companies?

Between the 1900s and the 1940s, patients flocked to what were called "prepaid physician groups," or "prepaid doctor groups."

Prepaid groups offered inexpensive health care because physicians acted as their own insurers. Patients paid a monthly fee directly to the group rather than to an insurance company. Physicians undermined their financial position if they either oversupplied services (as they do today) or if they rationed services. Ordering unnecessary tests and procedures drained away the group's resources and adversely affected physician pay, which was often tied to quarterly profits. But if patients were unhappy with their care, the group stood to lose paying patients.

Unlike today's medical group practices, prepaid groups were composed of doctors from various specialties. So rather than solely working with other general practitioners, GPs worked with surgeons, obstetricians and ophthalmologists. At the end of each day, the group's physicians met with one another to consult over tricky cases. Thus, chronically sick patients and individuals with several conditions or difficult-to-diagnose illnesses enjoyed one-stop medical care.

Many health care reformers, including those behind President Truman's failed 1948 universal care proposal, hoped to develop the medical economy around prepaid groups. Progressives believed that by federally funding prepaid groups, they could efficiently supply the entire population with comprehensive care.

Why Did the AMA Oppose Prepaid Doctor Groups?

As prepaid doctors groups gained in popularity, the AMA took notice and began organizing to combat them.

AMA leaders were afraid that self-insuring, multi-specialty groups would eventually evolve into health care corporations. They feared that this "corporate medicine" would render physicians mere cogs in a bureaucratic hierarchy.

So AMA officials threatened doctors working for or contemplating joining prepaid groups. Because AMA members occupied influential roles in hospitals and on state licensing boards, practitioners who refused to heed their warnings usually lost their hospital admitting privileges and medical licenses. These actions severely weakened existing prepaid groups and prevented physicians from establishing new ones.

But the AMA also vigorously opposed government involvement in health care. While they had great success defeating prepaid doctor groups, AMA leaders realized that that if they continued knocking down private attempts to organize health care, government officials would step in to manage the medical economy. Indeed, throughout the 1930s and 1940s, health care reform was a popular goal for progressive policymakers.

The Birth of the Insurance Company Model

In order to build up the private sector as a means for fighting government health care reform, AMA leaders designed the insurance company model.

AMA leaders decided that rather than allowing doctors to insure patients, only insurance companies would be permitted to offer medical coverage.

During the 1930s, insurance companies sold life insurance policies and worked with businesses to provide employee pensions. Insurance company executives had no interest in entering the health care field. But they reluctantly agreed to go along with the AMA plan in order to help physicians defeat nationalized medicine.

AMA officials believed they could keep corporate power separate from medicine by instituting a few rules. First, insurance companies were forbidden from financing multi-specialty physician groups. AMA officials insisted that physicians practice individually or in single-specialty partnerships. Second, the AMA banned the use of set salaries or per-patient fees. They instead required insurance companies to pay doctors for each and every service they supplied (fee-for-service payment). Finally, the AMA prohibited insurance companies from supervising physician work. Physician leaders concluded that these arrangements would protect their earnings and autonomy.

Unfortunately, the insurance company model fragmented care across numerous specialties and encouraged physicians and hospitals to practice without regard for financial resources. With a distant corporation footing the bill, there was little to prevent hospitals and physicians from ordering unessential tests and procedures for insured patients. Many patients with insurance received excessive medical services. Unwarranted surgeries—for example, medically unnecessary appendectomies—became a national crisis by the 1950s, and hospital admission rates increased far beyond what even the most innovative technologies called for.

Medicare Adopts the Insurance Company Model

From the 1940s on, the nation's health care system steadily developed around the faulty insurance company model. Though initially uneasy with one another, physicians and insurers worked together to strengthen and spread insurance company arrangements. They did so to demonstrate that the federal government need not interfere in health care. And their gambit worked: Physicians and insurers defeated attempts under Presidents Truman and Eisenhower to reform health care.

When federal politicians finally did intervene in health care with the passage of Medicare in 1965, the insurance company model had been developing for decades. Government agencies simply could not match the private economy's organizational capabilities. So, grudgingly, the health care reformers and progressive politicians behind Medicare built their program of government-funded health policies for the elderly around the insurance company model. Medicare's architects also appointed insurance companies to act as program administrators, to operate as intermediaries between the federal government and hospitals and physicians, a role that they have to this day.

Medicare's adoption of the insurance company model signaled its complete domination of US health care.

Predictably, health care prices skyrocketed. Even before Medicare's passage, politicians, journalists, and academics had been debating what to do about rising health care costs. Then Medicare brought millions of new elderly—and more sickly—patients into the system. Consequently, from 1966 through 1973, health care spending increased approximately 12 percent each year. Today, US medical care expenditures are the highest in the world, making up 18 percent of the nation's gross domestic product.

To control prices, insurers have gradually, over the course of many decades, implemented cost containment measures. These measures have required doctors to report their actions to insurers and increasingly seek insurer permission to perform medical services and procedures.

Insurers, once forbidden from supervising physician work, now act as managers, peering over the shoulders of doctors in a vain effort to counteract payment incentives that have created an oversupply of insured care.

Insurance Companies Maintain Their Position in the ACA

While the flaws of the insurance company model have become more evident, reforming the system has proven extremely difficult. Just look at the Affordable Care Act.

ACA planners attempted to undermine the insurance company model by proposing a public option—government-managed insurance that officials could deck out with generous benefits while subsidizing coverage to hold down policy prices. This strategy would allow the public option to outcompete and eventually destroy existing private-sector coverage. Opponents, including the AMA, viewed it as a step toward a government takeover of health care. Amid the intense political fighting, the public option was dropped, and the ACA was built around the insurance company model.

Thus, since the ACA's passage, premium prices have continued to climb and deductibles have increased. Insurers have scaled back the number of physicians and hospitals in their networks. At the same time, researchers question health care quality and service disparities.

Looking to the Future

Reacting to voters' frustration with this news, both presidential candidates have called for additional health care reforms. Reforms based on prepaid doctor groups hold the potential for bipartisan support.

Hillary Clinton is calling for a public option, which, if passed, would weaken the power of insurance companies. Clinton could use such a policy to reboot the prepaid group model.

Donald Trump advocates the repeal of the ACA and the sale of insurance across state lines. Republicans, citing fealty to market competition and consumer choice, could also rally around prepaid doctor groups.

With growing patient dissatisfaction and concern among physicians about insurance company dominance, prepaid groups could finally succeed.

6

What Are Medicare and Medicaid?
Nicole Galan

Nicole Galan is a registered nurse with ten years of experience caring for clients across the age/health spectrum, focusing on women's health and infertility issues. In addition to her clinical experience, she also writes health content for consumers.

Understanding the two current United States government health care programs, Medicare and Medicaid, can be confusing. In the following viewpoint, Nicole Galan, a medical professional, clearly explains the history of these programs, the issues they were created to address, and the difference between them. The services they provide and the eligibility requirements for receiving these services are also explained.

Medicaid and Medicare are two governmental programs that provide medical and health-related services to specific groups of people in the United States.

The two programs are very different, but they both come under the management of the Centers for Medicare and Medicaid Services. This is a division of the US Department of Health and Human Services.

President Lyndon B. Johnson created both Medicaid and Medicare when he signed amendments to the Social Security Act on July 30, 1965.

"What Are Medicare and Medicaid?" by Nicole Galan, Medical News Today, November 30, 2018. Reprinted by permission.

Medicaid is a social welfare, or social protection, program. Data from August 2018 show that it serves about 66.6 million people.

Medicare is a social insurance program that served more than 56 million enrollees in 2016.

Medicaid, Medicare, the Children's Health Insurance Program, and other health insurance subsidies represented 26 percent of the 2016 federal budget, according to the Center on Budget and Policy Priorities.

The Centers for Medicare and Medicaid Services (CMS) report that 91.1 percent of the US population had medical insurance in that year.

According to the 2017 US census, 67.2 percent of people have private insurance while 37.7 percent have government health coverage.

What Is Medicaid?

Medicaid is a means-tested health and medical services program for certain individuals and low-income households with few resources.

Primary oversight of the program happens at the federal level, but each state is responsible for:

- establishing its eligibility standards
- determining the type, amount, duration, and scope of its services
- setting the rate of payment for services
- administering its own Medicaid program

What Services Does Medicaid Provide?

Each state makes the final decisions regarding what their Medicaid plans provide, but they must meet some federal requirements to receive federal matching funds.

Medicaid does not directly provide people with health services. Instead, it reimburses healthcare providers for the care that they deliver to enrolled patients.

Not all providers need to accept Medicaid, so it is essential that users check their coverage before receiving care.

People who do not have private health insurance can seek help at a federally qualified health center (FQHC). These provide coverage on a sliding scale, depending on the person's income.

Centers must provide specific services, including:

- inpatient hospital services
- outpatient hospital services
- prenatal care
- vaccines for children
- physician services
- nursing facility services for people aged 21 years or older
- family planning services and supplies
- rural health clinic services
- home healthcare for people who are eligible for skilled nursing services
- laboratory and X-ray services
- pediatric and family nurse practitioner services
- nurse-midwife services
- FQHC services and ambulatory services
- early and periodic screening, diagnostic, and treatment (EPSDT) services for both children and adults under the age of 21 years

States may also choose to provide optional additional services and still receive federal matching funds. The most common of the 34 approved optional Medicaid services are:

- diagnostic services
- prescribed drugs and prosthetic devices
- optometrist services and eyeglasses
- nursing facility services for children and adults under the age of 21 years
- transportation services
- rehabilitation and physical therapy services
- dental care

Who Is Eligible for Medicaid?

Each state sets its own Medicaid eligibility guidelines.

The program aims to help people in low-income households, but there are other eligibility requirements, too. These relate to age, pregnancy status, disability status, other assets, and citizenship.

For a state to receive federal matching funds, it must provide Medicaid services to individuals who fall under certain categories of need.

For example, the state must provide coverage for some individuals who receive federally assisted income-maintenance payments and similar groups who do not receive cash payments.

The federal government also considers some other groups to be "categorically needy." People in these groups must also be eligible for Medicaid.

They include:

- children under the age of 18 years whose household income is at or below 138 percent of the federal poverty level (FPL)
- pregnant women with a household income below 138 percent of the FPL
- people who receive Supplemental Security Income (SSI)
- parents who earn an income that falls under the state's eligibility for cash assistance

States may also choose to provide Medicaid coverage to other, less well-defined groups who share some characteristics with those above.

These may include:

- pregnant women, children, and parents who earn an income above the mandatory coverage limits
- some adults and seniors with low income and limited resources
- people who live in an institution and have low income
- certain adults who are older, have vision loss or another disability, and have an income below the FPL

Universal Health Care

- individuals without children who have a disability and are near the FPL
- "medically needy" people whose resources are above the eligibility level that their state has set

Medicaid does not provide medical assistance to all people with low income and resources.

The Affordable Care Act of 2012 gave states the option to expand their Medicaid coverage.

In the states that did not expand their programs, several at-risk groups are not eligible for Medicaid.

These include:

- adults over the age of 21 years who do not have children and are pregnant or have a disability
- working parents with incomes below 44 percent of the FPL
- legal immigrants during their first 5 years of living in the US

Who Pays for Medicaid?

Medicaid does not pay money to individuals but sends payments to healthcare providers instead.

States make these payments according to a fee-for-service agreement or through prepayment arrangements, such as health maintenance organizations (HMOs).

The federal government then reimburses each state for a percentage share of their Medicaid expenditures.

This Federal Medical Assistance Percentage (FMAP) changes each year, and it depends on the state's average per capita income level.

The average reimbursement rate varies between 57 and 60 percent. Wealthier states receive a smaller share than poorer states, which can receive up to 73 percent of the money back from the federal government.

In the states that chose to expand their coverage once the Affordable Care Act became effective, more adults and families on low incomes became eligible because the new provision allowed enrolment at up to 138 percent of the FPL. In return, the federal government covers all of the expansion costs for the first 3 years and over 90 percent of the costs moving forward.

What Is Medicare?

Medicare is a federal health insurance program that pays for hospital and medical care both for people in the US who are older and for some people with disabilities.

The program consists of:

- two main parts for hospital and medical insurance (Part A and Part B)
- two additional parts that provide flexibility and prescription drugs (Part C and Part D)

Medicare Part A

Medicare Part A, or Hospital Insurance (HI), helps pay for hospital stays and other services.

In the hospital, this includes:

- meals
- supplies
- testing
- a semi-private room

It also pays for home healthcare, such as:

- physical therapy
- occupational therapy
- speech therapy

However, these therapies must be on a part-time basis, and a doctor must consider them medically necessary.

Part A also covers:

- care in a skilled nursing facility
- walkers, wheelchairs, and some other medical equipment for older people and those with disabilities

Payroll taxes cover the costs of Part A, so a person does not usually have to pay a monthly premium. However, anyone who has not paid Medicare taxes for at least 40 quarters will need to pay it.

Medicare Part B

Medicare Part B, or Supplementary Medical Insurance (SMI), helps pay for specific services.

These include:

- medically necessary physician visits
- outpatient hospital visits
- home healthcare costs
- other services for older people and those with a disability
- preventive care services

For example, Part B covers:

- durable medical equipment, such as canes, walkers, scooters, and wheelchairs
- physician and nursing services
- certain vaccinations
- blood transfusions
- some ambulance transportation
- immunosuppressive drugs after organ transplants
- chemotherapy
- certain hormonal treatments
- prosthetic devices
- eyeglasses

For Part B, people must:

- pay a monthly premium, which was $134 per month in 2018
- meet an annual deductible of $183 a year, before coverage begins

Premiums might be higher or lower depending on the person's income and Social Security benefits.

Enrollment in Part B is voluntary.

Medicare Part C

Medicare Part C, also known as Medicare Advantage Plans or Medicare+ Choice, allows users to design a custom plan to suit their medical needs more closely.

Part C plans provide everything in Part A and Part B, but may also offer additional services, such as dental, vision, or hearing.

These plans enlist private insurance companies to provide some of the coverage. However, the details will depend on the program and the eligibility of the individual.

Some Advantage Plans team up with HMOs or preferred provider organizations (PPOs) to deliver preventive healthcare or specialist services. Others focus on people with specific needs, such as individuals living with diabetes.

Medicare Part D

This prescription drug plan was a later addition in 2006. Several private insurance companies administer Part D.

These companies offer plans that vary in cost and cover different lists of drugs.

To participate in Part D, a person must pay an additional fee called the Part D income-related monthly adjustment amount. The fee will depend on the person's income.

In many cases, the amount will come out of the person's Social Security check. However, others will get a bill from Medicare instead.

Services that Medicare Does Not Provide

If Medicare does not cover a medical expense or service, Medigap plans can provide supplemental coverage for it.

Private companies also offer Medigap plans.

Depending on the individual plan, Medigap may cover:

- copayments
- coinsurances
- deductibles
- care outside of the country

If a person has a Medigap policy, Medicare will first pay the portion that it will cover, and then Medigap will pay the rest.

To have a Medigap policy, a person must have both Medicare Part A and Part B and pay a monthly premium.

Medigap policies do not cover prescription drugs. A person must have a Part D plan for that coverage.

Who Is Eligible for Medicare?

To be eligible for Medicare, an individual must meet one of the following requirements:

- being at least 65 years old
- being under 65 years old and living with a disability
- being any age with end-stage renal disease or permanent kidney failure that needs dialysis or a transplant

They must also be:

- a US citizen or permanent legal resident for 5 continuous years
- eligible for Social Security benefits with at least 10 years of contributing payment into the system

Dual Eligibility

Some people are eligible for both Medicaid and Medicare. Currently, 8.3 million people have both types of cover, including over 17 percent of Medicaid enrollees. Seniors with a low income and people with disabilities may be eligible for both.

Provisions vary depending on the US state in which a person lives.

Who Pays for Medicare?

Most of the funding for Medicare comes from:

- payroll taxes that the Federal Insurance Contributions Act (FICA) collects
- the Self-Employment Contributions Act (SECA)

Usually, the employee pays half of this tax, and the employer pays the other half.

This money goes into a trust fund, which the government uses to reimburse doctors, hospitals, and private insurance companies.

Additional funding for Medicare services comes from premiums, deductibles, coinsurance, and copays.

If health spending continues as it is, national health spending is likely to rise by 5.5 percent each year from 2017 to 2026. In 2016, government health spending represented 17.9 percent of Gross Domestic Product (GDP). In 2026, experts expect that it will account for 19.7 percent of GDP.

7

Medical Bankruptcy and the Economy

Kimberly Amadeo

Kimberly Amadeo has twenty years of experience in corporate economic analysis and business strategy. She received an M.S. in management from the Sloan School of Business at M.I.T. Amadeo is the US economy expert for the Balance and has been writing for Dotdash/About.com since 2006. She covers economic and business news, and explains how the economy affects everyone.

One of the biggest causes of personal bankruptcy in the US is medical bills. High medical costs can force families to mortgage homes, go into severe debt, and lose their ability to work. In this viewpoint, Kimberly Amadeo argues that declaring bankruptcy due to medical bills is not the best decision, and that managing existing medical conditions and maintaining savings to use in the event of a serious medical issue are better choices.

Medical bills were the biggest cause of US bankruptcies, according to a CNBC report. It estimated that 2 million people were adversely affected. A popular Facebook meme said that 643,000 Americans go bankrupt each year due to medical costs. President Obama, in his 2009 State of the Union address, said that a medical bankruptcy occurred every 30 seconds. That's 1 million bankruptcies in a year.

"Medical Bankruptcy and the Economy," by Kimberly Amadeo, The Balance, a part of Dotdash Publishing Family, February 3, 2019. Reprinted by permission.

Rising health care costs make these statistics seem credible. But why are they so different? And what is the actual impact of medical bankruptcies on the economy? Most importantly, what's the best way for you to avoid becoming one of those statistics?

Medical Bankruptcy Facts

One reason why the estimates are so different is that they were done in different years. Those years were following the Great Recession. As a result, bankruptcy rates of all kinds skyrocketed. Consumer bankruptcies rose from 775,344 in 2007 to 1.5 million in 2010. By 2017, they'd fallen to 767,721.

That's one reason why President Obama's estimate was so high. In 2009, there were 1.4 million bankruptcies. Obama based his calculation on a 2009 Harvard study coauthored by his assistant, Elizabeth Warren. It said 62.1 percent of all bankruptcies were because of medical bills. The researchers interviewed those who filed for bankruptcy between January and April 2007. It expanded medical causes to include:

- Those who mortgaged a home to pay medical bills.
- Those who had medical bills greater than $1,000.
- People who lost at least two weeks of work due to illness.

Several scientists criticized the researchers for being too broad in including those last two reasons.

Even so, Obama's calculations were a little high. Multiply 1.4 million bankruptcies by the Harvard study's 62.1 percent, and you get 877,372 bankruptcies created by medical bills.

In 2011, researchers Tal Gross and Matthew Notowidigbo found that out-of-pocket medical costs caused 26 percent of bankruptcies. Their study only looked at low-income debtors.

In 2013, two studies created wildly different conclusions. The most widely reported was done by NerdWallet Health. The researchers based their estimates on the 2009 Harvard study. They excluded the bankruptcies due to job losses from medical problems. The researchers declared that 57.1 percent was more accurate.

Later that year, CNBC reported that NerdWallet found that medical bills caused 646,812 Americans to declare bankruptcy. CNBC extrapolated that to everyone in their household. The average household has three people, which translates to 2 million people affected. The Facebook meme summarized the same article to arrive at its estimate of 643,000 medical bankruptcies. The mythbuster Snopes used the study to disprove the Facebook meme.

Also in 2013, bankruptcy attorney Daniel A. Austin found that up to 26 percent of bankruptcies were primarily due to medical costs. He only counted large medical costs as a major of cause bankruptcy. These large costs were more than 50 percent of the respondent's total debt or more than 50 percent of his/her income. Total personal bankruptcies in 2013 were 1,038,720. Multiply 26 percent by total bankruptcies, and you get 270,067 bankruptcies.

In 2015, the Kaiser Family Foundation found that medical bills made 1 million adults declare bankruptcy. Its survey found that 26 percent of Americans age 18 to 64 struggled to pay medical bills. According to the US Census, that's 52 million adults. The survey found that 2 percent, or 1 million, said they declared bankruptcy that year.

In 2017, Debt.org found that people aged 55 and older account for 20 percent of total filings. That number has doubled since 1994. Even with assistance from Medicare, the average 65-year-old couple faces $275,000 in medical bills throughout retirement.

Who to Believe

Researchers disagree on how much medical bills cause bankruptcies. The biggest problem in answering the question is that those filing for bankruptcy aren't required to state the reason. As a result, estimates are based on surveys. The methodology differs from study to study. It depends on how the researchers and the survey respondents define medical debt.

Second, a variety of factors cause bankruptcies. Most people with medical debt have other debt. They may also have low income, little savings, and job losses. That makes it difficult to determine whether the bankruptcy was because of medical debt alone. For example, the Kaiser Family Foundation study found that only 3 percent said their bankruptcy was because of medical debt. But another 8 percent said it was because of a combination of medical and other debt.

It also found that the insured were a bit more likely to declare bankruptcy (3 percent) than the uninsured (1 percent). Most probably thought their insurance protected them from medical costs. They weren't prepared to pay for unexpected deductible and coinsurance costs. Almost a third weren't aware that a particular hospital or service wasn't part of their plan. One-in-four found that the insurance denied their claims.

How did those with insurance wind up with so many bills? After high deductibles, co-insurance payments, and annual/lifetime limits, the insurance ran out. Other companies denied claims or just canceled the insurance.

How to Avoid Medical Bankruptcy

It's not a good idea to file for bankruptcy to discharge medical bills. For one thing, a bankruptcy stays on your record for 10 years. You may not be able to rent an apartment, get an auto loan, or buy a home. Some employers would reject your job application for that reason.

In some states, you may lose your home. For example, Nebraska only protects $12,500 in home equity from seizure. In total, you could lose $100,968 in assets. The biggest loss is in Delaware, where you could lose $125,745 on average.

Also, bankruptcy is expensive. Average costs are from $1,500 to $3,000 for a Chapter 7 filing with a lawyer. Chapter 13 average costs are from $3,000 to $4,000 with an attorney. Those are national average costs. The costs could be much higher in urban areas.

The best way to avoid medical bankruptcy is to prevent or manage chronic diseases like diabetes.

High medical bills from accidents can't be avoided. For those situations, a financial cushion is a must. Sock away three to six months of expenses in a savings or money market account. Only a third of Americans have more than $1,000 in savings.

As the research shows, health insurance won't completely protect you. Many people were bankrupted by high deductibles and other out-of-pocket expenses. You should have at least the amount of your deductible in savings.

8

Is the ER Better Than Primary Care?
Robert Wood Johnson Foundation

The Robert Wood Johnson Foundation is the only foundation in the US dedicated to health. It supports research and programs targeting some of the country's most pressing health issues, including substance abuse and improving access to quality health care. It also feels that America's health should not focus on only health care. Where people live, learn, work, and play also affects their health.

For people without regular family physicians to address their health issues, the hospital emergency room might be their only source for medical treatment, even when those conditions are not life threatening. Many lower-income patients actually prefer ER visits to seeing a regular doctor in an office setting. But because ER visits are generally very expensive, these non-emergency visits are one of the biggest targets of health care reform.

One of the drivers of high health care costs in the United States is the use of emergency rooms (ER) for preventable conditions by patients who generally come from the most vulnerable populations. Estimated to cost as much as $30.8 billion a year in a recent *Health Affairs* study, avoidable ER use is a primary target for experts seeking to reduce health care costs.

To achieve this goal and "generate system-wide savings, experts need to listen to patients and address their concerns about the cost,

---

"Low-Income Patients Say ER Is Better Than Primary Care," Robert Wood Johnson Foundation, July 9, 2013. Copyright 2013. Robert Wood Johnson Foundation. Used with permission from the Robert Wood Johnson Foundation.

quality and accessibility of outpatient care," said Shreya Kangovi, MD, a Robert Wood Johnson (RWJF) Clinical Scholar (2010-2012) supported in part by the US Department of Veterans Affairs.

Kangovi's new study reports that current approaches to getting patients from low-socioeconomic groups to seek preventive and primary care in physicians' offices or accountable care organizations instead of hospitals are often ineffective.

"Our findings suggest that these efforts could backfire by making hospitals even more attractive to these patients. We also debunk the notion that people from these groups abuse the emergency room for no reason and need to be taught how to use it properly."

Insurance Status Is Not the Key

Working from literature that shows ER usage patterns are not necessarily linked solely to insurance status, Kangovi explained that she "wanted to find a way to address the ongoing disparities" she saw in her patient population. "To do so, I designed the study so that we could talk with patients whose voices are seldom heard in policy discussions."

Kangovi and her team conducted one-on-one interviews with 64 patients, ages 18-to-64, from two urban Pennsylvania hospitals. Forty of them met the criteria to be included in the study. They were uninsured or insured by Medicaid. The respondents, who were 90 percent African American, also lived in one of five Philadelphia zip codes where more than 30 percent of the residents had incomes below the poverty level.

The results were published in the July *Health Affairs* cover story "Understanding Why Patients of Low Socioeconomic Status Prefer Hospitals Over Ambulatory Care."

"We asked them: 'What are some of the reasons you might prefer to come to the emergency room rather than your primary care doctor's office or clinic?'" Kangovi said. "The interviews were conducted by a community health worker who was a member of their community, so there was more of a trusting relationship."

Study respondents (both the insured and uninsured) explained that they consciously chose the ER because the care was cheaper, the quality of care was seemingly better, transportation options were more readily accessible, and, in some cases, the hospital offered more respite than a physician's office.

Excessive Barriers to Primary Care

"As a physician, I found the results very disturbing. We discovered that our system is just riddled with barriers to primary care," Kangovi said. Patient voices taken from study interviews tell the story best:

- **Convenience.** "You must call on the same day to set up a [primary] care appointment … whenever they can fit you in." This open-access scheduling resulted in people taking days off from work and still being unable to see a doctor. It also made it impossible for many to access transportation covered by Medicaid because the transport arrangements had to be made 72 hours in advance. Late hospital hours also made care more available.
- **Cost.** "I don't have a co-pay in the ER, but my primary [physician] may send me to two or three specialists and sometimes there is a co-pay for them. Plus there's time off from work to go to several appointments."
- **Quality.** "The [primary care doctor] never treated me or my husband aggressively to get blood pressure under control. I went to the hospital and they had it under control in four days. The [physician] had three years." This patient was one of many who expressed far more trust in the quality of hospital care.

Shelter from the Storm

In order to better understand study participants' needs, Kangovi sorted them into two groups—those with five or more acute care episodes a month (group A) and those with less than five acute episodes a month (group B).

"The patients in group A had often gone through extraordinary trauma and were more likely to say that a traumatic event set off a cycle of social dysfunction, mental illness, and disability that drove their repeated hospital visits," Kangovi explained.

"The group B patients were most often highly functional caregivers for social networks strained by poverty and illness. These people often put off caring for themselves. Both groups had extremely eloquent and valid reasons for avoiding preventive care, waiting to get sick and choosing emergency care," she added.

Creating a National Model for Change

Acknowledging that this research has some limitations, such as the small size of the study sample, Kangovi intends to encourage other researchers to focus on vulnerable patients.

"I used the health services research training I gained as a Clinical Scholar, as well as the incredible support I received from my Clinical Scholar program mentors including my co-authors David Grande, MD, MPA, and Judith Long, MD, to address problems I saw from a public health and eventual policy perspective," Kangovi said. "We plan to disseminate the study strategy."

"We learned that the patients are the experts in the flaws in our health care system and the people we need to listen to," Kangovi advised. "You hear the term 'patient-centered care,' well you have to talk to patients to create that care. Right now, they are telling us that we are creating a maze of hoops and hurdles that are driving them out of primary care and into the hospital."

9

It's Inevitable, Single Payer Health Care Is Coming to America

Ed Dolan

Edwin G. Dolan holds a PhD in economics from Yale. He has taught in the United States at Dartmouth, the University of Chicago, George Mason University, and Gettysburg College. He has also taught economics in several European countries, including Central European University in Budapest, the University of Economics in Prague, and fifteen years of annual courses at the Stockholm School of Economics in Riga.

The bold messaging of conservatives has made Americans fear the health care systems of our peer nations, systems that produce equivalent care a half the cost (or less) of ours—but cover everybody. America's march to universal coverage began with Medicare (1965) and Medicaid (1966). In the following viewpoint, Ed Dolan draws the conclusion that single payer insurance will come to America. The United States is alone among advanced economies in not having a single payer health care system with universal coverage. It is, however, already much closer to such a system than most people realize, and the current round of Republican health care reforms, if enacted according to plan, will bring it even closer. Yet there is no reason to fear the single payer future.

"Single Payer Healthcare Is Coming to America. It's Inevitable," by Ed Dolan, Fabius Maximus, March 17, 2017. https://fabiusmaximus.com/2017/03/17/single-payer-healthcare-will-come-to-america. Licensed under CC BY 4.0 International.

The True Scope of Government in Our Healthcare System

The federal government already operates three large healthcare systems, Medicare, Medicaid, and the Veterans Administration. Each of the first two is comparable in size to the single payer systems of most European countries. If we categorize healthcare expenditures by the type of primary payer, the three big federal programs accounted for roughly a third of all spending in 2015, according to data from the Centers for Medicare and Medicaid Services (Figure 1).

To get a true picture of the government role in healthcare, though, we need a different perspective. If we categorize expenditures by the source of the funds, instead of the type of payer, the government share of spending is much larger. Partly that is because state and local governments account for 17 percent of all healthcare spending, not fully reflected in the chart above. Also, that chart hides the extent to which federal tax expenditures finance much of our ostensibly private health insurance. According to data from the Tax Policy Center, deductions and exclusions of health insurance premiums and related tax breaks cost the federal government some $250 billion in revenue in 2015—as big a burden on the federal budget as if Uncle Sam wrote a check for that amount.

Deductibility of employer healthcare expenditures account for about three-fifths of total tax expenditures. The remainder come in the form of exclusions of Medicaid benefits from declared income, deductibility of insurance for self-employed individuals, tax breaks for some kinds of out-of-pocket costs, and other items. If we categorize healthcare expenditures according to the ultimate source of funds rather than the primary payer, we find that government budgets account for over half of all spending, as Figure 2 on the next spread shows.

Figure 1. US Healthcare Expenditures by Primary Payer Percent of All Healthcare Spending, 2015

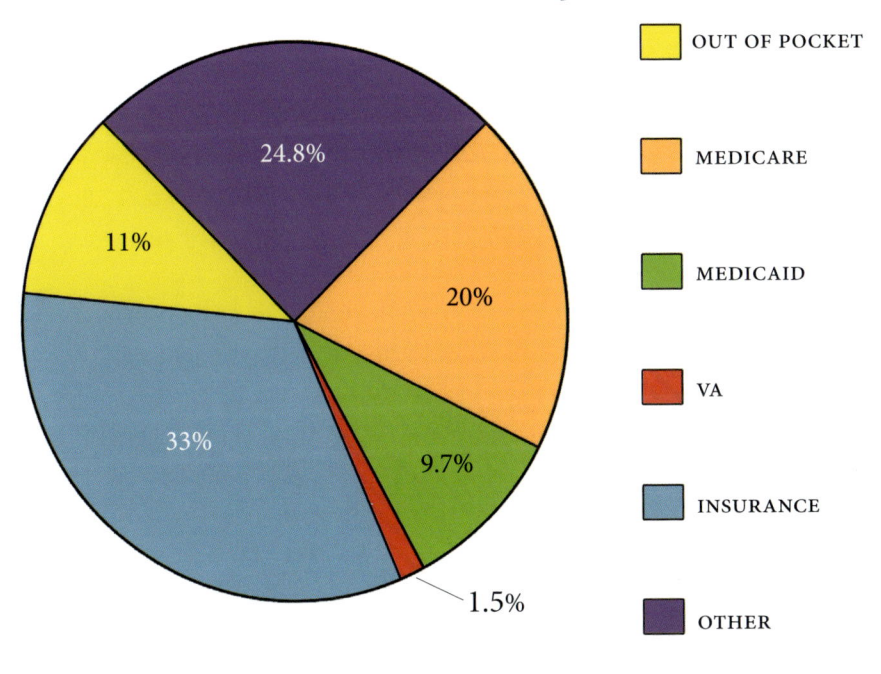

- OUT OF POCKET: 11%
- MEDICARE: 20%
- MEDICAID: 9.7%
- VA: 1.5%
- INSURANCE: 33%
- OTHER: 24.8%

Source: CMS.gov

Our Faltering Private Insurance System

Both the Affordable Care Act (ACA or "Obamacare") and the current Republican repeal-and-replace law, the American Health Care Act (AHCA), attempt to salvage what is left of private healthcare finance. Unfortunately, the two pillars of private healthcare, employer-sponsored insurance and individual insurance plans, are beyond saving.

The individual insurance market is failing because too large a share of health care risks are inherently uninsurable. Two conditions must hold for a real insurance market to work. First, the risks in question must be fortuitous, that is, predictable statistically but not predictable for any particular individual. Second, premiums

Universal Health Care

Figure 2. US Healthcare Expenditures by Source of Funds Including Tax Expenditures, Percent of All Healthcare Spending, 2015

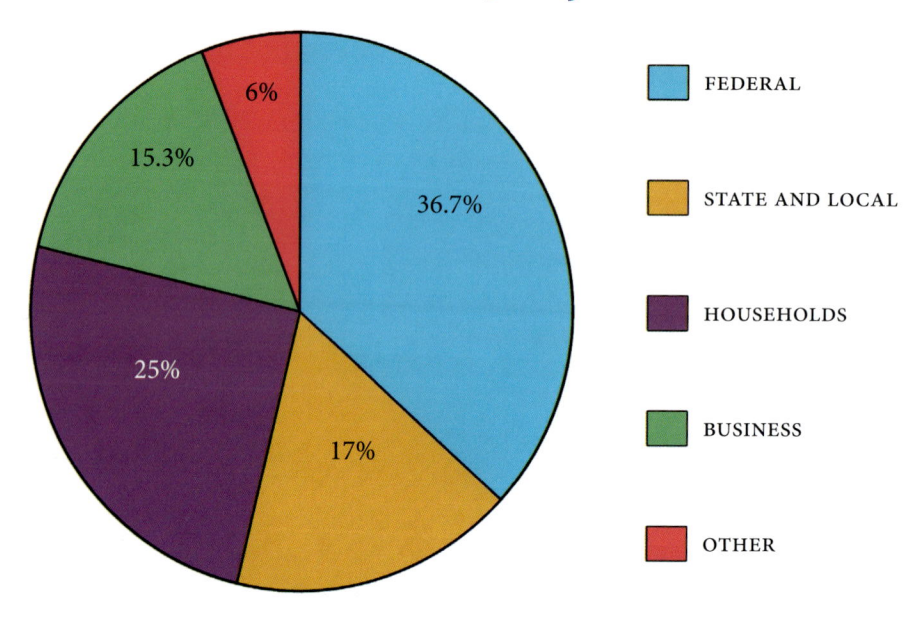

- FEDERAL — 36.7%
- STATE AND LOCAL — 17%
- HOUSEHOLDS — 25%
- BUSINESS — 15.3%
- OTHER — 6%

Source: **Tax Policy Center**

must be high enough to cover claims and administrative expenses, yet still affordable to the customer.

Neither condition holds for individual health insurance. The principal reason is that a tiny share of the population accounts for the great bulk of all healthcare spending. The next chart, based on data from the Kaiser Family Foundation, shows that the top 10 percent of households account for two-thirds of all personal healthcare spending, and the top 5 percent for half of all spending. The majority of these high spenders have one or more chronic conditions that keep their spending high year after year (Figure 3).

The skewed pattern of spending poses a dilemma for policymakers: If they allow insurance companies to refuse to issue

Figure 3. Concentration of Healthcare Spending in US Economy

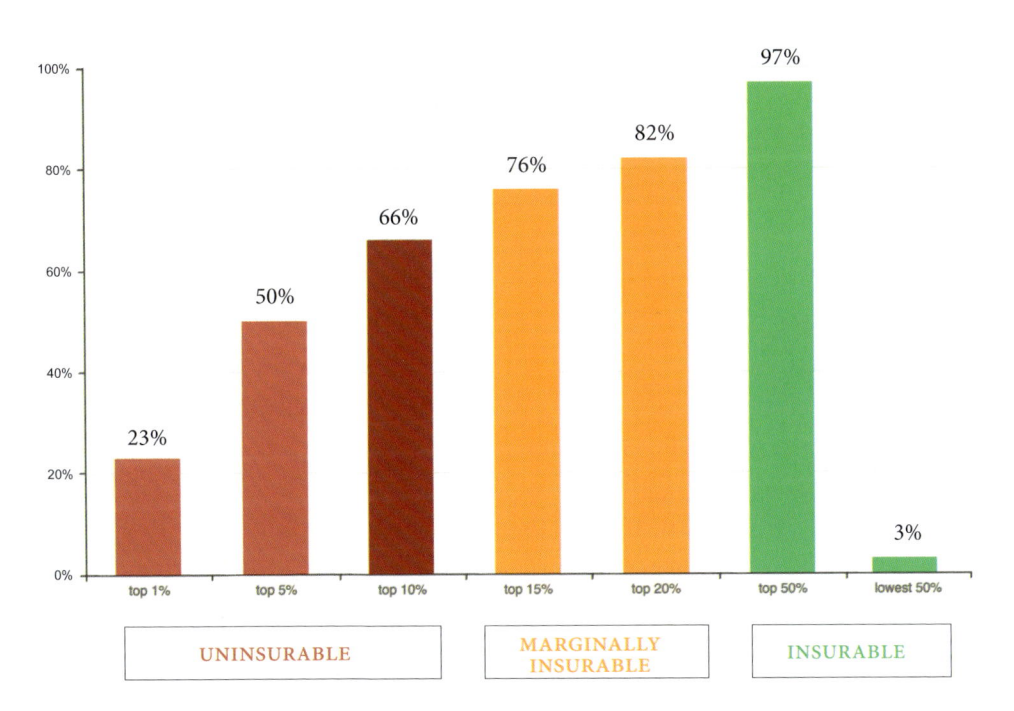

Group	Percentage
top 1%	23%
top 5%	50%
top 10%	66%
top 15%	76%
top 20%	82%
top 50%	97%
lowest 50%	3%

UNINSURABLE: top 1%, top 5%, top 10%
MARGINALLY INSURABLE: top 15%, top 20%
INSURABLE: top 50%

Source: **Kaiser Family Foundation**

policies to people with pre-existing conditions, the people most in need of medical care will not be able to buy policies. If they insist on guaranteed issue, then the presence of high spenders in the risk pool pushes up premiums for everyone. As that happens, relatively healthy people drop out of the pool, pushing claims and premiums higher still for those who remain. As losses mount, insurers begin to drop out, too, until the system collapses.

Both the ACA and the ACHA opt for guaranteed issue. That sounds good politically, since everyone knows a neighbor or relative with a pre-existing condition even if they don't have one themselves. Ultimately, though, guaranteed issue is an unsustainable policy that threatens the whole individual insurance market with a "death spiral." The ACA is already showing early signs of such a spiral, and, as I explained in this earlier post, the ACHA seems designed to make things worse rather than better.

Meanwhile, employer-sponsored health insurance has problems of its own. First, it works much better for large corporations than for small businesses. Most small firms simply do not have enough employees to constitute an affordably insurable risk pool. Second, economists believe that over time, employees end up bearing the cost of healthcare benefits through lower pay. Rising employer healthcare costs are thus a major contributor to the stagnation of wages. Third, the fear of losing insurance coverage makes people reluctant to give up jobs that are otherwise unsuitable — reluctant to try something new or start a business of their own. This "job lock," in turn, reduces labor mobility and makes the economy less able to respond to shocks from new technologies and changing patterns of trade.

For these reasons, job-linked health insurance has been gradually dying for some time now. According to another report from the Kaiser Family Foundation, from 1999 to 2014, the share of the nonelderly population covered by employer-sponsored insurance fell from 67 percent to 56 percent. If the ACHA, as planned, repeals the ACA's employer mandate, the downward trend will pick up speed. The Congressional Budget Office estimates that over ten years, 7 million employees will lose employer-sponsored insurance as a result of the AHCA. Republican plans for sharp reductions in corporate tax rates would produce an unintended blow to employer-sponsored insurance, since the incentive of tax deductibility would suddenly be worth less.

What Lies Ahead?

Despite the best of intentions, the ACA has been unable to save private-sector health insurance in either its individual or employer-sponsored form, and the AHCA, if enacted, will only accelerate the decline. That leaves two possibilities. Either the share of the population without effective access to the healthcare system will begin to rise again, or the government share of the national healthcare budget will continue to grow.

In the short run, Republicans may opt for reduced coverage, but I doubt if that will prove politically acceptable, once it actually starts to hit home. Looking at CBO projection of decreased coverage is one thing; waking up in the morning to find that Aunt Sally can't get her chemo or Uncle John can't get his bypass surgery is another thing altogether. At that point, some kind of single payer system will be the only option left.

And really, it is not such a bad alternative. A revealing report from the Commonwealth Fund ranks US healthcare eleventh out of eleven against those of ten high-income countries, all with single payer systems. US healthcare is at the top in terms of cost, and at the bottom in terms of efficiency and equity. And no, contrary to the scare stories, other countries do not use death panels or endless waiting periods to ration care. The United States ranks in the middle of the pack on measures of timeliness of care, although it is the worst of the eleven in terms of cost-related limitations on access.

So get used to it. We, too, could free up a good chunk of our national income on healthcare, reduce medical insecurity, and cut the high administrative costs of our fragmented and overlapping healthcare systems. Single payer healthcare is coming. Stop fighting it and start figuring out how to make it work here, as it does elsewhere.

10

What Is "Single-Payer" Health Care?
Meridian Paulton

Meridian M. Paulton is a research assistant in domestic policy studies at the Heritage Foundation's Institute for Family, Community, and Opportunity. She focuses on a variety of health policy issues and has contributed to analysis on Medicare, Medicaid, mental illness, and the State Children's Health Insurance Program.

"Single-payer" health care is a term that is often heard in the debate about universal health care and how it should be implemented in the United States. But many people do not know what the term means. In the following viewpoint, Meridian Paulton explains what single-payer health care is, its pros and cons, and various models for how it could be used within the health care system.

Leading Democrats in the US Senate and more than half of Democrats in the US House of Representatives have voiced support for "single-payer" health care—a full government takeover of American health care.[1] Its promise of simplicity strikes a chord with Americans who are frustrated with high costs and complex payment arrangements. This sentiment is amplified by the fact that some Americans face additional trouble accessing care if they are sick or low-income. Single-payer advocates claim that full government control of health care is the answer, and they argue

"What Is 'Single-Payer' Health Care?" by Meridian Paulton, The Heritage Foundation, November 29, 2018. Reprinted by permission.

that such a system would deliver superior quality care for everyone at lower costs than current public and private arrangements.

Upon closer examination, however, these claims are greatly exaggerated. Government-controlled health care would substantially raise taxes for all Americans. Moreover, it would slash payments to medical providers, resulting in less access to quality care for millions of Americans. The experiences of the United Kingdom and Canada offer a cautionary lesson of government-run health care. Under these systems, the government rations care—resulting in delays and denials for its citizens.

Leading Single-Payer Proposals: Medicare for All

The term "single-payer" is an umbrella term for a variety of approaches to government-funded health care.[2] In its purest form, it refers to a universal system in which the government itself becomes the national health insurer. With few exceptions, it typically supplants or abolishes previously existing public and private health coverage.

The most prominent proposal for government-controlled health care is S. 1804, the Medicare for All Act of 2017, introduced by Senator Bernie Sanders (I–VT).[3] This proposal would create a national health insurance program covering all US residents.[4] Coverage would include 10 benefit categories and eliminate nearly all cost sharing, making care "free" at the point of service. It would prohibit employer-sponsored coverage and all other private insurance, except for non-covered benefits or services.[5] The proposal would also eliminate nearly all existing public coverage arrangements, most notably Medicare, Medicaid, and the State Children's Health Insurance Program (CHIP).[6]

Following a four-year transition period, the federal government would enroll all residents covered under current private and public arrangements (as well as those currently uninsured) into the new, federal insurance program.[7] Under this scenario, 164 million Americans would lose their employer-sponsored insurance; 17 million Americans would lose their individual-market insurance; and 75 million Americans would lose Medicaid or CHIP. Ironically, even though the title of the bill is "Medicare for All," over 57 million elderly and disabled Americans would lose their existing Medicare coverage and instead be enrolled in the new program.[8] In short, almost all Americans would lose the health care coverage they have today.

The Sanders plan suggests financing the cost of the program in part through a combination of new payroll and income taxes.[9] The plan would impose a set of specialized taxes—including taxes on investments and dividends—and target tax-rate increases on Americans making over $250,000. The proposal also assumes significant savings from reductions in administrative costs and substantial cuts in payment for doctors, hospitals, and other medical professionals. Under the Sanders proposal, doctors and other medical professionals would receive Medicare-level reimbursements, and the proposal would severely restrict any private contracting between doctors and patients outside the government program.[10] Health spending in the new government program would be subject to a global health care budget and governed by an elaborate regulatory system of centralized decision making in the US Department of Health and Human Services.[11]

There is a similar Medicare for All proposal in the US House of Representatives, H.R. 676, the Expanded and Improved Medicare for All Act of 2017. The bill was originally introduced by Representative John Conyers (D–MI) and is currently sponsored by Representative Keith Ellison (D–MN).[12] While broadly similar, this proposal varies on some points from Senator Sanders' bill.

- The House bill does not provide a transition period between systems, while Sanders' offers a four-year transition period.[13]
- The House bill permits anyone arriving at a medical facility to receive care: They are presumed covered under the plan, though they must submit an application for coverage.[14] Sanders' bill does not include this provision.

- The House bill also includes long-term care in the list of covered Medicare-for-All services, while Sanders keeps long-term care in the Medicaid program.[15]
- The House bill does not include any cost sharing, while Sanders' bill includes small copays for prescription drugs.[16]
- The House bill bans for-profit, investor-owned medical facilities, while the Sanders plan does not.[17]
- While the House bill is silent on private contracting, the Sanders proposal specifies that providers may opt-out of Medicare for All (though private insurance is banned).[18]
- Under the House bill, individual facilities and providers would receive global (fixed) budgets, while the Sanders plan sets the budget only at the national level.[19]
- Finally, the House bill proposes a combination of revenue sources, including a payroll tax, while the Sanders bill does not specify his revenue sources in the bill itself (other than current spending).[20] Sanders does, however, provide revenue suggestions in a separate document from the bill and proposes a variety of funding sources—but primarily relies upon a combined payroll tax and income-related premium equal to 11.5 percent of income.[21]

The High Cost of Government-Run Health Care

Health policy analysts from across the ideological spectrum have examined the potential cost of the Sanders' proposal. While the estimates vary methodologically, they all consistently show the proposal would require substantial federal tax increases and could impose major deficits, depending on actual incurred revenue. The Urban Institute, a widely respected liberal-leaning think tank, estimates that Senator Sanders' plan would cost $32 trillion in new federal spending over 10 years. Yet Urban finds that the proposed combined payroll and income tax of 11.5 percent would bring in only $15.3 trillion of the needed $32 trillion—leaving a 10-year deficit of more than $16.7 trillion.[22]

Universal Health Care

Economist Ken Thorpe of Emory University, a former adviser to President Bill Clinton, estimates the 10-year cost of Sanders' plan at $24.7 trillion.[23] Like the Urban Institute, Professor Thorpe finds that Senator Sanders' tax proposal would be insufficient to cover the full cost of the proposal. He estimates a shortfall of nearly $1.1 trillion per year. Professor Thorpe estimates that the tax level required to cover the true cost would need to be about 20 percent in combined new payroll and income taxes.

Analysts at the Center for Health and Economy estimate a 10-year cost of up to $44 trillion. This estimate assumes the Sanders proposal offered coverage equivalent to current "platinum"-level plans offered in the individual and small-group health insurance markets. The Center's analysts also find that Senator Sanders' revenue proposal would be insufficient and would result in a deficit of up to $2.11 trillion in the program's first year.[24]

More recently, Dr. Charles Blahous, Senior Fellow at the Mercatus Center at George Mason University and former public trustee of Social Security and Medicare, estimates a 10-year cost of $32.6 trillion. In his estimate of the Sanders bill, he notes that "doubling all currently projected federal individual and corporate income tax collections would be insufficient to finance the added federal costs of the plan."[25]

Reduced Access to Care in Single-Payer Systems

With insufficient revenue, single-payer systems usually depend on government officials holding firm to the global health care budgets that restrict national spending or imposing payment regulations, reductions, or price controls on medical goods and services. The Sanders bill includes both approaches to control national health spending.

US policymakers can look to international experience on how such systems work in practice. The British National Health Service (NHS) and Canadian health systems, both single-payer systems, explicitly ration health care—creating access problems for patients.

What Is "Single-Payer" Health Care?

Wait Lists

Wait lists are a significant problem in the Canadian system. In 2017, Canadians were on waiting lists for an estimated 1,040,791 procedures.[26] Physicians reported that only about 11.5 percent of patients "were on a waiting list because they requested a delay or postponement," meaning much of the remainder was systemic failure.[27] Often, wait times are lengthy. For example, the median wait time in Canada for arthroplastic surgery (hip, knee, ankle, shoulder) ranges from 20 weeks to 52 weeks.[28]

Cancellations

In the British NHS, cancellations are common. In 2017, the NHS canceled 84,881 elective operations in England for non-clinical reasons on the day the patient was due to arrive.[29] The same year, the NHS canceled 3,845 urgent operations in England.[30] Episodes of frequent illness tend to aggravate this problem. During the 2018 flu season, for example, the NHS canceled 50,000 "non-urgent" surgeries.[31]

Poor Performance

In the United States, the Veterans Administration (VA) health program and the Indian Health Services (IHS), both government-run health care programs, have a history of poor performance.[32] A 2015 report revealed that in the VA, as many as 238,000 veterans may have died while they were waiting for care. Curiously, in spite of these shocking revelations, the Sanders' bill would preserve the VA program, along with the troubled IHS.[33]

Professional Problems

Not only patients, but also doctors would face a more difficult practice environment under a single-payer program. Earlier this year, the *British Medical Journal* published a study of general practitioners who have left practice or are planning to leave.[34] The most commonly cited reasons were the lack of professional autonomy, administrative challenges, and increasingly unmanageable workloads.

Conclusion

American policymakers should reject "single-payer" proposals such as Medicare for All. Although the promise of "free" care may be attractive, in reality such a system would cost most taxpayers more than they pay today. It would take control from patients and their doctors and put it in the hands of government politicians and bureaucrats.

The international track-record on single-payer plans confirms that this consistently leads to poor access to care—and even to denial of care. In short, single-payer would have the effect of higher costs and reduced access to care for many patients. Instead, Congress should seek to reduce costs and increase access to care for Americans through proposals that empower patients and doctors.[35]

Notes

1. For a list of Senate supporters, see "Cosponsors: S.1804; 115th Congress (2017–2018)," https://www.congress.gov/bill/115th-congress/senate-bill/1804/cosponsors (accessed November 5, 2018). For a list of House supporters, see "Cosponsors: H.R. 676; 115th Congress (2017–2018)," https://www.congress.gov/bill/115th-congress/house-bill/676/cosponsors (accessed November 5, 2018).

2. Signe Peterson Flieger, "What We Talk About When We Talk About Single Payer," *Health Affairs*, September 19, 2017, https://www.healthaffairs.org/do/10.1377/hblog20170919.062040/full/ (accessed November 15, 2018).

3. Medicare for All Act, S. 1804, 115th Congress, 1st Sess. For more information, see Robert E. Moffit, "Government Monopoly: Senator Sanders' 'Single-Payer' Health Care Prescription," Heritage Foundation Backgrounder No. 3261, July 27, 2018, https://www.heritage.org/health-care-reform/report/government-monopoly-senator-sanders-single-payer-health-care-prescription.

4. S. 1804, § 102.

5. Ibid., § 801.

6. The plan would retain the Veterans Administration Health Program and the Indian Health Service.

7. S. 1804, § 1002.

8. "Employer-sponsored" and "individual market" categories from National Association of Insurance Commissioners data, accessed through Mark Farrah Associates, http://www.markfarrah.com (accessed August 16, 2018). For Medicaid and CHIP information, see Centers for Medicare and Medicaid Services, "Updated February 2017: Medicaid & CHIP December 2016 Application, Eligibility, and Enrollment Data," https://www.medicaid.gov/medicaid/program-information/downloads/updated-december-2016-enrollment-data.pdf (accessed August 20, 2018). For Medicare information, see Centers for Medicare and Medicaid Services, "Medicare Enrollment: Medicare Advantage & Other Health Plans," 2016, https://www.cms.gov/Research-Statistics

What Is "Single-Payer" Health Care?

-Data-and-Systems/Statistics-Trends-and-Reports/Dashboard/Medicare-Enrollment/Enrollment%20Dashboard.html (accessed August 20, 2018).

9. Bernie Sanders, "Options to Finance Medicare for All," https://www.sanders.senate.gov/download/options-to-finance-medicare-for-all (accessed August 20, 2018). See also Expanded and Improved Medicare for All Act, H.R. 676, 115th Congress, 1st Sess., § 211.

10. S. 1804, §§ 202 and 303, respectively.

11. S. 1804, § 401.

12. H.R. 676. The bill will soon be sponsored by Representative Pramila Jayapal (D–WA). See Kimberly Leonard, "Pelosi Faces Conflict with Her Caucus Over 'Medicare for All,'" *The Washington Examiner*, November 10, 2018, https://www.washingtonexaminer.com/policy/healthcare/pelosi-faces-conflict-with-her-caucus-over-medicare-for-all (accessed November 26, 2018).

13. H.R. 676, § 101, and S. 1804, § 1002.

14. H.R. 676, § 101(c).

15. H.R. 676, § 102, and S. 1804, § 204.

16. H.R. 676, § 102, and S. 1804, § 202.

17. H.R. 676, § 103(a).

18. S. 1804, § 303.

19. H.R. 676, § 201, and S. 1804, § 601.

20. H.R. 676, §211, and S. 1804, § 701.

21. Sanders, "Options to Finance Medicare for All."

22. John Holahan, Lisa Clemans-Cope, Matthew Buettgens, et al., "The Sanders Single-Payer Health Care Plan," The Urban Institute, May 2016, https://www.urban.org/sites/default/files/alfresco/publication-pdfs/2000785-The-Sanders-Single-Payer-Health-Care-Plan.pdf (accessed August 20, 2018).

23. The Thorpe estimate excludes a proposed long-term care program. See Kenneth E. Thorpe, "An Analysis of Senator Sanders' Single Payer Plan," January 27, 2017, https://www.scribd.com/doc/296831690/Kenneth-Thorpe-s-analysis-ofBernie-Sanders-s-single-payer-proposal (accessed October 10, 2017).

24. The Center for Health and Economy, "Medicare for All: Leaving No One Behind," May 1, 2016, http://healthandeconomy.org/medicare-for-all-leaving-no-one-behind (accessed August 19, 2018).

25. Charles Blahous, "The Costs of a National Single-Payer Healthcare System," Mercatus Center, July 2018, https://www.mercatus.org/system/files/blahous-costs-medicare-mercatus-working-paper-v1_1.pdf (accessed August 20, 2018).

26. Bacchus Barua, "Waiting Your Turn: Wait Times for Health Care in Canada," The Fraser Institute, 2017, https://www.fraserinstitute.org/sites/default/files/waiting-your-turn-2017.pdf (accessed August 19, 2018).

27. Ibid.

28. Ibid.

29. Carl Baker, "NHS Key Statistics: England, October 2018," House of Commons Library, May 21, 2018, http://researchbriefings.files.parliament.uk/documents/CBP-7281/CBP-7281.pdf (accessed November 19, 2018).

30. Ibid.

31. Laura Donnelly, and Henry Bodkin, "NHS Hospitals Ordered to Cancel All Routine Operations in January as Flu Spike and Bed Shortages Lead to A&E Crisis," *The Telegraph*, January 3, 2018, https://www.telegraph.co.uk/news/2018/01/02/nhs-hospitals-ordered-cancel-routine-operations-january/ (accessed August 20, 2018).

32. John O'Shea, "Reforming Veterans Health Care: Now and for the Future," Heritage Foundation Issue Brief No. 4585, June 24, 2016, https://www.heritage.org/health-care-reform/report/reforming-veterans-health-care-now-and-the-future.

33. For a discussion of problems in the Indian Health Service, see the US Government Accountability Office, Indian Health Service: Actions Needed to Improve Oversight of Quality of Care, Report to Congress, GAO–17–181, January 9, 2017, https://www.gao.gov/products/GAO-17-181 (accessed October 24, 2017).

34. Anna Sansom, Rohini Terry, Emily Fletcher, Chris Salisbury, Linda Long et al., "Why Do GPs Leave Direct Patient Care and What Might Help to Retain Them? A Qualitative Study of GPs in South West England," *British Medical Journal*, Vol. 8, No. 1, https://bmjopen.bmj.com/content/8/1/e019849 (accessed September 18, 2018).

35. The Health Care Choices proposal offers Congress a starting place toward such a goal. Its intent is to reduce costs, increase access, and provide patients—not the government—with more control over their health care. For more details see Health Policy Consensus Group, "The Health Care Choices Proposal: Policy Recommendations to Congress," June 19, 2018, https://www.healthcarereform2018.org/wp-content/uploads/2018/06/Proposal-06-19-18.pdf (accessed September 18, 2018).

Is Universal Health Care Still Unthinkable in America?

Adam Gaffney

Dr. Adam Gaffney is a pulmonologist and critical care physician, as well as a writer and researcher. He teaches medicine at the Harvard University Medical School. As a writer, he focuses on the policy, politics, and history of health care. His articles have appeared in the Washington Post, *the* Guardian, *the* New Republic, *the* Los Angeles Review of Books, USA Today, Salon, *the* Nation, CNN .com, *and* US News & World Report. *He is also the author of the book* To Heal Humankind: The Right to Health in History.

The idea of universal health care in the United States used to be an issue on the edges of politics until the advent of the Affordable Care Act under President Obama. In the following viewpoint, Dr. Adam Gaffney argues that history has shown that bringing universal health care into the spotlight of politics means that there will be many obstacles and arguments ahead. However, it might be possible to finally find a way to pay for and implement health care for all US citizens.

Barack Obama dropped a bombshell into the healthcare debate roiling the Democratic party last Friday. "Democrats aren't just running on good old ideas like a higher minimum wage," he

"Universal Healthcare Was Unthinkable in America, But Not Any More," by Adam Gaffney, Guardian News and Media Limited, September 16, 2018. Reprinted by permission.

Universal Health Care

said, "they're running on good new ideas, like Medicare for All …" His endorsement made headlines, and for a good reason: until recently, real universal healthcare had long resided on the margins of the American political discourse. Obama's announcement, then, was yet one more indication that this idea—also called single-payer healthcare—had migrated to the mainstream. The shift is an encouraging development for proponents, to be sure, but there is also cause for caution: as history shows, formidable political obstacles and pitfalls lie ahead.

It is difficult to overstate how far single-payer has recently moved. Consider, for a moment, where things stood after Democrats took the presidency and both houses of Congress in 2008. "The White House and Democratic leaders have made clear," the *Washington Post* reported the following year, "there is no chance that Congress will adopt a single-payer approach … because it is too radical a change." Single-payer supporters didn't even have a seat at the table (and some were arrested when they showed up anyway).

Following the passage of the Affordable Care Act, however, several developments pushed single-payer to the fore. First, although Obamacare expanded coverage to some 20 million people—achieving much good—it raised hopes that universal healthcare would be achieved while failing to deliver it: some 29 million remain uninsured today, while many more face onerous deductibles, restrictive insurance networks, surprise bills, unaffordable medications, medical bankruptcies and disruptions in care with every change in insurance plan.

Next, there was the 2016 election of Donald Trump, which made it obvious that Republicans lacked even a semi-serious alternative. Congressman Paul Ryan's long-awaited ACA repeal bill was mostly a mechanism to transfer healthcare dollars from the poor into the savings accounts of the rich, and it seemed to satisfy no one except for wealthy donors.

Finally, there was a marked progressive shift within the Democratic party, beginning with the 2015-16 presidential primary campaign. Former secretary of state Hillary Clinton opposed single-payer, saying it would "never, ever" happen, but it was central to the platform of Vermont senator Bernie Sanders. Sanders lost the primary, of course, but he advocated better ideas.

Obama's endorsement of single-payer on Friday (despite having previously said something similar) is therefore tantamount to a major shift in the Overton window, reflecting years of activism by single-payer supporters as well as a historic intra-party shift.

Today, in primary contests across the country, progressive Medicare-for-All proponents are ousting more centrist and establishment candidates—Alexandria Ocasio-Cortez's surprise primary win in New York's 14th congressional district being the most popular example. At the same time, public support has soared: a recent Reuters poll found that 70.1% want Medicare for All, including 84.5% of Democrats. One might even argue that for people who want a job as a Democratic politician, in other words, supporting single-payer is nearly becoming a prerequisite.

None of this is to say, however, that enacting it legislatively—even with a new government in power—will be easy. We have, after all, been down this road before.

A Concept Older Than Medicare

As some have noted, Obama wasn't quite right to call Medicare for All a "new" idea: on the contrary, Medicare for All is a concept older than Medicare itself. Medicare came about after the defeat of single-payer—then called "national health insurance"– during the Truman administration. The campaign against it was led by the American Medical Association (AMA), which famously did it in with the help of a cutting-edge public relations firm that waged an unremitting campaign of cutthroat red baiting (drug firms also lent support).

But something similar is brewing today. As the *Hill* reported last month, a new anti-single-payer group has recently formed—drawing together the lobbying muscle of both insurance companies and big pharma—and it's spoiling for a fight. Single-payer poses an existential threat to insurers, after all, and the industry's coming PR blitz could make the famed "Harry and Louise" TV ad campaign of the 1990s—credited with helping sink Bill Clinton's healthcare reform—look like an undergraduate's mediocre final project for a marketing course.

This is a major obstacle, but a surmountable one: all great reforms in history, including Medicare itself, had to overcome powerful opponents. Yet a second potential pitfall lies ahead: despite all that has happened, politicians could still walk away from single-payer—probably by watering "improved Medicare for All" down into something unrecognizable. And again, something similar has happened before.

After the AMA's defeat of national health insurance, its architects narrowed their proposal to cover just seniors; this became known as "Medicare". However, the idea was that the Medicare approach could later be used to cover everyone. A push was made to realize this universal vision within a few years of the implementation of the program, and indeed, had things happened somewhat differently, some sort of national health insurance legislation could have been achieved in the 1970s.

Ultimately, however, the movement disintegrated—in large part the consequence of a historic rightward political turn that culminated in the election of Ronald Reagan. Fatefully, this was also the moment when the Democratic party abandoned national health insurance, instead embracing a private-insurance based alternative built on Richard Nixon's reform proposal, which the ethically compromised Republican president had offered as a counter to single-payer.

Brick-by-brick, the campaign for national health insurance was rebuilt. In the late 1980s, for instance, the organization I serve—Physicians for a National Health Program—was formed, and its proposal for what was newly called "single-payer" became the blueprint for HR 676, the Improved and Expanded Medicare for All Act that was first introduced in Congress in 2003. That year, it had only 38 co-sponsors, but today HR 676 is supported by an unprecedented 123 lawmakers, or some two-thirds of the Democratic caucus. Meanwhile, Bernie Sanders' companion bill in the Senate, the Medicare for All Act of 2017, has achieved 16 co-sponsors (his previous bills had zero).

The Future of Single-Payer

The danger, however, is that even with the prospects of these bills on the rise, Democrats could turn away from the essence of the vision. Already, some are aiming to mutate Medicare for All into something vastly inferior—for instance, into an expansive "public option"-type program that would retain a major role for private insurers (eg the Center for American Progress's confusingly labelled "Medicare Extra-for-All"). But to achieve real universal healthcare, Democrats can't afford to repeat the mistakes of the past and flee to a private-insurance based reform a second time around. Medicare for All must remain what it is today—how it is detailed in a bill like HR 676—if it is to mean anything at all: fully public national health insurance providing comprehensive, universal coverage to the entire nation.

Wilbur Cohen, a chief architect of both Truman-era national health insurance and Medicare, recognized this when he asserted that private insurance companies should have no role in a Medicare for All system, although it was not yet called that. "[O]nce the Federal Government decides that everybody is going to be insured," he put it in 1977, "there is no need for a private insurance company to go out and sell coverage … using private insurance agencies to achieve the public responsibility seems to me to be wasteful and unnecessary, imposing an additional cost … without any essential advantage."

His point is even more salient today: private insurance companies add only fragmentation and cost, something we can't afford as we work to provide everyone in the nation with comprehensive first-dollar coverage.

For the first time in a generation, the realization of a right to healthcare—through implementation of a single-payer system—

is on the horizon. But achieving it requires not repeating the mistakes of history. It means somehow countering a staggeringly rich corporate opposition while at the same time preserving the essence and the details of the vision—one which, by necessity, leaves no room for the waste and avarice of the private insurance industry. It is a formidable task, but one that has never seemed so winnable.

12

7 Reasons Why Universal Health Care Won't Work in the US

Kevin Mercadante

Kevin Mercadante is a freelance personal finance blogger and the author of the personal finance blog OutOfYourRut.com. He has backgrounds in both accounting and the mortgage industry.

In the following viewpoint, Kevin Mercadante argues that universal health care will not work in the United States. The author provides seven specific reasons why it won't. These reasons include the idea that doctors will leave their profession because they will no longer earn enough income and that taxes will increase substantially to fund health care at the high rates of medical care in this country, as well as other points based on the unique American institutions and mindsets.

In one of last week's posts, Could You Afford an $1875 COBRA Payment Every Month?, reader John touched on single-payer health insurance in a comment. I confessed that I'm coming around to the idea. But I've been doing some thinking since the comment exchange, and have come to the conclusion that universal healthcare won't work in the US.

Don't get the wrong idea—while I think that it could work just swell in theory, it's the execution where I think it will fall apart. I was able to think of seven reasons why universal healthcare

"7 Reasons Why Universal Healthcare Won't Work in the US," by Kevin Mercadante, OutOfYourRut.com. Reprinted by permission.

won't work in the US. None of them require too much thought to imagine.

1. The Already High Cost Base of US Healthcare

According to the Centers for Disease Control (CDC), US healthcare costs reached $3.2 trillion—that's *-rillion* with a "T," not a "B"—in 2015. That represented a 5.8% increase over 2014, as well as a 17.8% share of the entire US economy. It works out to be $9,990 per person. All future projections see these numbers rising faster than the growth of the economy.

That's a bunch of numbers, but I want to focus on the 17.8% of the US economy that healthcare consumes.

According to the Organisation for Economic Co-operation and Development, the average percentage of total gross domestic product (GDP) consumed by the average developed country in the world is just 8.9%.

That figure is for 2013, but having researched this information over the years, that percentage has held throughout the years. It's the US where the percentage is rising most dramatically on a year-to-year basis.

Here's the problem with that statistic…Europe and Canada are managing universal healthcare systems at about half the cost of the US on a per capita basis. As most of us know, costs don't scale the way other relationships do. Too costly is too costly, and there's no way around that.

To roll out a universal healthcare system with the type of cost structure that currently exists in the US would doom the system to failure from the very beginning. The US healthcare system is simply too bloated to be scaled back and managed. As well, the entire industry functions on the assumption of ever higher revenues. It will take years to reverse that dynamic, under the assumption that it's even possible.

2. Doctors Will Exit the Field

One of the biggest reasons why universal healthcare won't work in the US is that there's no way it can work without severely restricting reimbursements to healthcare practitioners. We can look to Medicare and Medicaid as examples of this process already in motion.

As well, government being government, it won't just fund healthcare, it will regulate it. Or more precisely, it will over-regulate it, to the point of exhaustion and failure.

I saw firsthand how the regulation process works. When I was in the mortgage business, I watched as the government encouraged overly aggressive lending practices, in the name of increasing homeownership. But when it was obvious that strategy was doomed to failure, they went too far in the other direction, and virtually shut down the industry.

When government gets involved, processes turn into convoluted flow charts. Government tries to address all ills and potentialities, and in the process it creates built-in conflicts and gray zones. Just look at the federal tax code for guidance. And while we're at it, just look at Obamacare. It will be considerably worse with universal healthcare.

As doctors begin to realize that their incomes are being reduced, and their day-to-day operations are being closely monitored and controlled (I mean, much more than they are already), we'll see a mass exodus from the profession.

It will likely take the form of early retirements, and fewer students going to medical school (and less willing to take on the six-figure debt levels needed to attend). The end result will be fewer doctors, and still higher fees for the services that are available.

3. The High Cost of Malpractice Insurance

This is something I learned about firsthand when I was working in public accounting. Accounting firms work with a lot of medical practices, and you get to see the expense side of a doctor's existence.

It's often true that the single biggest expense the practice has is malpractice insurance. We're not talking a few thousand dollars a year here—it can easily be well over $100,000 per year, per doctor.

You can bet your house and your bank account that Congress is not going to do anything to limit malpractice litigation. That ruling body is comprised primarily of lawyers, and there's no way to get them to support any kind of restrictions. Just look at all of the commercials for ambulance chasers on daytime TV. It's big business, and it's one of the primary drivers of the legal industry in the US.

No matter what anyone thinks, we can't have universal healthcare without serious tort reform. If it doesn't happen, and universal healthcare is still implemented, that'll be another major reason contributing to doctors exiting the field.

4. The Uniquely American Pay-any-Price Mentality

America is the land of the unlimited. For the first nearly 200 years of our existence as a nation, we had abundant everything. Abundant land, workers, markets, energy, food—you name it.

Back in the 1960s, then President Lyndon Johnson even promised we could have it all. It was the guns-and-butter promises that we could both maintain the welfare state at home (his "Great Society"), while carrying on the Cold War against the Soviet Union and fighting the war in Vietnam.

It's been the mentality in America ever since. A big part of it is supported by the monetary system, which probably not one American in 100 actually understands. The United States government issues the US dollar. It serves as the global reserve currency, which is to say that virtually every other currency in the world is tied to the dollar. This gives the US the "exorbitant privilege" of paying its foreign obligations in its own currency.

It's Also the Reason Why We Have Inflation

All countries in the world create inflation by printing money. It's the kind of thing that you can do easily with paper and digital money. But the more money that's put into circulation, the higher prices eventually become.

Americans became very comfortable with the unspoken reality that our government can pay any price. Sure, about every two years we're treated to a political battle over cutting the budget, but it's really just theater. Neither party is going to balance the budget, because it doesn't matter. The government can print or borrow as much money as it needs for whatever it wants to do. Whatever treasury debt the government can't sell in the open market, will be purchased by the Federal Reserve, which is empowered to literally print money out of thin air.

The point is, Americans have become very comfortable with this arrangement. The sky's the limit, and that's what we expect from the healthcare industry. We want the best health care money can buy, and we want as much of it as we can get. At the same time, our expectation is that we won't have to pay for it.

That's a recipe for disaster. Government is careful to maintain pretty inflation numbers. But should we get universal healthcare, it's entirely possible that the financial printing presses will be rolling. When that happens, not only will we be paying higher prices for healthcare, but also for everything else we need to buy.

That brings up Reason #5…

5. Taxes Will Explode

While the government loves some inflation—it's even a stated target of the Federal Reserve—they don't want too much of it.

Too much inflation means that the government loses control of the currency. And lots of bad political and economic outcomes can result from that. As a result, you can count on your taxes going higher after universal healthcare is implemented. And a lot higher at that.

Universal Health Care

Medicare is already costing the country $675 billion on an annual basis. Medicaid is costing $574.2 billion per year. That's a total of about $1.25 Trillion per year.

Now imagine if the federal government has to cover all $3.2 Trillion of the US healthcare system—or whatever inflated number that will be in the future. That means that the government will need to raise an additional $2 trillion to cover those costs. Rest assured they're not going to print and borrow $2 trillion per year just so that everyone can have cheap healthcare.

No, They'll Raise Taxes—Substantially

Currently, total federal tax revenues run at about $3.25 trillion. If we add an extra $2 trillion to the government's expenditures, that will mean that the government will need to collect roughly 62% more in taxes than they are right now.

And that's just to keep the current budget deficit from going any higher than it is right now.

Imagine that your taxes are going up by 62% so that you can have government-funded health insurance. And not just your federal income taxes, but also the FICA tax, including the half of that tax that your employer pays on your behalf. Do you still want that deal?

I'm pretty sure that I don't. And we haven't even factored in future increases in healthcare spending, or the negative effects that the next recession will have on government revenues. What it all means is that the numbers above are the best case scenario. Things can probably only get worse, not better.

6. Any US Universal Healthcare System Will NOT Be Based on the European or Canadian Models

The US recently was ranked #11 out of 11 countries for quality of healthcare. I'm always dubious about these international ratings, because the pattern seems to be that they intentionally attempt to make the US look bad. But that doesn't mean that we don't have a lot to learn from other countries and how they operate.

But that's the problem. Americans have always viewed themselves as something unique under the sun. We tend to think of all things foreign as being corrupt, and completely unworkable within the context of the American system.

But given what a wreck we've turned our healthcare system into, we could use a lot of instruction from foreign countries. After all, they're able to provide universal healthcare at about half the per capita cost that we do. That means something big that we're choosing to ignore.

Unfortunately, it's unlikely that we will look at the universal healthcare systems in other countries for guidance. Instead, we'll come up with our own convoluted system that pretends that no other universal strategy has ever been successfully implemented.

It's been said that a giraffe is a horse designed by Congress; my guess is that any universal healthcare system devised by the US government will look a lot more like a wounded giraffe than a healthy horse.

7. Medicare Will Be the Likely Model for Universal Healthcare in the US

Rather than rely on universal healthcare models currently working in Canada and Europe, it's far more likely that we'll get a system that will be based largely on an expansion of the existing Medicare system.

Just like the health insurance that most of us carry now, Medicare doesn't pay all of your medical bills. For example, under Medicare Part B, you must pay 20% of outpatient services costs, after you pay your annual deductible. For this reason, many people who are on Medicare also maintain a Medicare supplement, that pays the costs that Medicare doesn't. There's a premium for that as well.

Translation: don't assume that universal healthcare will mean the end of premiums!

In fact, there is a monthly premium of $134 per person for Part B coverage, and possibly more for Part D (prescription drug coverage). And remember, these monthly premiums are not factored into the current portion of the FICA tax that's used to pay for Medicare. It's an additional cost to participants.

An expansion of Medicare to the general population would almost certainly include these premiums, in addition to higher income taxes. And that's before factoring in the additional costs that will occur when the 74 million people who are currently enrolled in the Medicaid program are rolled into the national plan with its upgraded benefits.

And worth noting is the fact that some healthcare providers don't want to even participate in the Medicare program, because of limits on reimbursements for services. How an expansion of the program to universal level will play out in this way is open to debate.

Closing Thoughts…

Don't get the wrong idea, I'm not looking for ways to torpedo the idea of universal healthcare. I'm even glad that John brought the topic up. Given the high COBRA payments that my family is currently paying each month, as well as the fact that I'm self-employed, we would certainly benefit from a universal system—maybe more so than most families.

In addition, I've often thought that universal coverage would make it much easier for people to change jobs or go into business for themselves. Universal coverage would mean they wouldn't have to worry about losing employer subsidized coverage.

For all of those reasons I'd love to see a workable universal healthcare system implemented in the US. But based on the realities of the current system and common expectations, I think it's likely that we'll get something that's even more dysfunctional than what we have now.

What are your thoughts on universal healthcare? Canada and Europe have it, in fact most countries in the world have it—but do you think that it can work in the US? And if so, how could it overcome the seven problems I've listed?

13

The Affordable Care Act: Past, Present, and Future

Gilbert Berdine

Dr. Gilbert Berdine is an associate professor of internal medicine at the Texas Tech University Health Sciences Center (TTUHSC) and a faculty affiliate with the Free Market Institute. His research interests include the application of economics to health care delivery and consumption.

In the following viewpoint, Gilbert Berdine discusses the Affordable Care Act (ACA), its origins, its current state, and what may happen to it going forward. He shows that the ACA was not intended to be a health insurance, but rather a subsidy, program, and that current political arguments may result in continuing or repealing the program. It is an expensive program, but it may provide lessons for creating universal health care in the United States.

The Affordable Care Act (ACA) was passed in 2010. This was arguably President Obama's signature piece of legislation and is commonly referred to as Obamacare. As politicians are wont to do, many promises were made. The most infamous promise was, "If you like your health care plan, you can keep it."[1] This was so obviously untrue that PolitiFact made it the 2013 Lie of the Year.[2] This promise was not directed at Medicare beneficiaries,

"The Affordable Care Act: Past Promises, Current Debates, Future Directions," by Gilbert Berdine, Southwest Respiratory and Critical Care Chronicles, 01/2018. http://pulmonarychronicles.com/index.php/pulmonarychronicles/article/view/434/956. Licensed under CC BY-SA 4.0 International.

since these people were generally happy with Medicare. Rather this promise was directed at people with employer based private health insurance. It was a promise that was doomed to fail given the structural features of the ACA.

The ACA was sold to the public as health insurance, but it had features that were incompatible with insurance. The ACA was a subsidy to two groups of people. The first group includes those who are insurable but who cannot afford actuarially sound insurance premiums. These would be the working poor and indigent. The second group consists of people who are uninsurable due to pre-existing conditions. Rather than having a risk of medical expenses that can be shared with others with similar risks, they have certain costs that must be paid but exceed their ability to pay.

The only feature that insurance has in common with a subsidy is that beneficiaries pay less in premiums than the costs of a claim. Insurance is able to do this because the risk of a claim is shared among many people. Nobody has to sacrifice anything to pay an insurance claim. A subsidy, on the other hand, must be paid by others who do not receive the benefits. In the case of the ACA, the subsidies are paid from general tax revenue.

Insurance that retains risk stratification has incentives for everyone to minimize their risk as people who take prudent steps to reduce risk qualify for a lower premium commensurate with their reduced risk. An example would be a health insurance policy that offers a reduced premium to non-smokers. Subsidies are received by people who do not see the costs; they have no incentives to reduce risk. This is known as moral hazard. The subsidized only have incentives to qualify for the subsidy. These incentives tend to have perverse economic effects. An example would be someone who is able to work but refuses in order to keep income below some arbitrary threshold to qualify for the subsidy. In some cases the value of the subsidy is greater than the value of the extra income that is declined irrespective of the extra time and effort necessary to earn the extra income.

The two main goals of the ACA were to decrease the number of uninsured people in the US and to lower health care costs. It should have surprised no one that the ACA was successful in the first goal, because subsidies always increase the quantity of transactions, all other things being equal.[3] The second goal should have been a red flag, however, since subsidies always increase the price, all other things being equal.[3] President Obama promised multiple times that premiums would decrease by $2,500 per year.[1] While some have argued that insurance premium increases have moderated since the ACA,[4] and others have argued that premium increases have dramatically increased since the ACA,[5] nobody claims that insurance premiums are decreasing.

Figure 1 [not shown] has important information relevant to the past, present, and future challenges for the ACA. I will return to this figure during discussion of the future trends, but for now, Figure 1 illustrates that health care expenditures are rising for private "insurance" as well as for public programs. Just as subsidies lead to increases in health care prices for Medicare and Medicaid, subsidies are responsible for rising health care prices in the so-called private sector. The insurance companies received, until recently, government subsidies to participate in the ACA exchanges. The other form of subsidy is the subsidy for pre-existing conditions. By making risk stratification for pre-existing conditions illegal, the average expected risk is less than the expected risk for those with pre-existing conditions and greater than the expected risk for those without pre-existing conditions. This subsidy from those without pre-existing conditions to those with pre-existing conditions has two major effects on the composition of the risk pool. Those with pre-existing conditions have an incentive to buy insurance at the subsidized rate, but those without pre-existing conditions have an incentive to take their chances without insurance and pay out of pocket for medical expenses as they arise. The Individual Mandate was created to force those without pre-existing conditions to pay higher premiums than were justified for their risk in order to subsidize those with pre-existing conditions. The Individual Mandate has been very unpopular and many have decided to pay penalties rather than buy insurance.[6] As healthy people opt out, the remaining risk pool has greater risk which leads to higher insurance premiums which escalates the incentive for healthy people to opt out. This is what is known as an insurance death spiral—which is a nice segue into the present state of the ACA debate.

The past year has seen important debates about the ACA. Repeal of the ACA was a major campaign promise by Republicans in general and President Trump in particular. The Republicans failed twice to get enough votes to repeal and replace the ACA. In general the public favors coverage of those with pre-existing conditions; individuals are just not interested in paying for this feature. The public opposes the Individual Mandate. While public support has kept the ACA from being repealed, the funding of the ACA subsidies to insurance companies has been decreased by presidential directive. Furthermore, the recently passed Tax Reform bill repeals the Individual Mandate for the ACA. Even before these changes, insurance companies were leaving the ACA marketplace exchanges. A major story in 2016/2017 was the departure of both Aetna and United Healthcare from the ACA exchange marketplaces.[8] These departures have left large portions of the US with only one carrier.

Earlier this year, the *New York Times* claimed that Obamacare was not in a death spiral.[9] This claim relied on estimates from the Congressional Budget Office (CBO), which assumed no major structural changes going forward. The *Washington Post* noted that elimination of the Individual Mandate could initiate an insurance death spiral and graphically explained how this could happen.[10] A few months ago, President Trump ended subsidies paid to insurance companies used to lower insurance costs for low income people. The *New York Times* now notes, "Without the subsidies, insurance markets could quickly unravel. Insurers have said they will need much higher premiums and may pull out of the insurance exchanges created under the Affordable Care Act if the subsidies were cut off. Known as cost-sharing reduction payments, the subsidies were expected to total $9 billion in the coming year and nearly $100 billion in the coming decade."[11] The death spiral issue is also made more likely by the elimination of the Individual Mandate in the recently passed Tax Reform bill. The future of ACA depends on whether individuals with pre-existing conditions will receive some new form of subsidy.

The possible futures for ACA include some form of repeal and/or replace, an incremental expansion of ACA type subsidized "insurance" exchanges, or some kind of universal coverage. Repeal and/or replace appear to have stalled and are unlikely. The Individual Mandate was eliminated. It seems likely that the debate over ACA will now become a debate over some form of universal coverage.

The *New England Journal of Medicine* championed possible futures with universal coverage in a recent issue with two articles, "Which Road to Universal Coverage"[12] and "How to Think about Medicare for All."[13] Neither article deals with the problems of how to pay for these programs. Everyone would prefer to have health care vs. not having health care. Advocates of government subsidized health care either do not realize or do not mention, however, that nobody would prefer having health care vs. having all other possible things. Otherwise, people would voluntarily choose health care over all of their other options and this discussion would be unnecessary. Free health care has unlimited demand; it is a fiscal black hole. Fantasy proposals of universal health care envision a world where everyone is devoting 100% of their efforts to satisfy the unlimited demands of health. This is a nightmare rather than a utopia. "Which Road to Universal Coverage?" explains away this fiscal problem with a single sentence: "A national health care budget would cap spending on included services."[12] It is somewhat contradictory that an article on universal coverage describes a "universal" coverage that is capped or limited.

So-called universal coverage is rationing by political means rather than rationing by the market. The market lets individuals decide when they prefer something else vs. the next incremental purchase of health care. Neither "Road to Universal Coverage" nor "Medicare for All" provides details on which services will not be covered or which people will be denied which services. "Which Road to Universal Coverage?" acknowledges that people "would have to believe that the national health budget would selectively purge useless or low-benefit care but not impair beneficial care or advances in medical technology."[12] This would indeed be a suspension of disbelief for any health care provider who has spent hours trying to obtain home oxygen or non-invasive ventilation for needy patients when the patient does not fit neatly into one of Medicare's checkboxes. Under universal coverage, rationing decisions would be made by the same people who literally lose billions of dollars[14] or who were responsible for the VA scandal.[15]

[There is] another problem with these universal coverage proposals. Government health care systems spend more per patient than private health care systems, yet we are supposed to believe (without any evidence at all) that shifting patients from private care to government care will cost less. Advocates of government subsidized health care never seem to acknowledge that subsidies ALWAYS make goods and services more expensive than they otherwise would be.

The 2017 Medicare Trustees Report has some eye-opening figures.[16] In calendar year 2016, Medicare covered 56.8 million beneficiaries at a cost of $678.7 billion ($12,829 per beneficiary). Although the so-called "revenues" to the trust fund are listed at $710.2 billion, that revenue figure includes $319.2 billion transferred from General Revenue. General Revenue is the government budget that is in deficit every year. Medicare is not pay as you go; rather Medicare borrows from the future without any expectation that the loan will ever be repaid.

In 2016, the US spent 17.9 percent of all economic output on health care.[6] Advocates of universal coverage want this figure to be higher. The problem with these proposals is they offer no mechanism to determine how much is too much. There are no restraints on the production of health care necessary to permit the production of other things.

"Medicare for All" justifies the huge tax increases necessary to pay for the program as a means to address income inequality. "'Medicare' for All offers politicians a way to squarely address the issue. It would lift a substantial financial burden from low and middle-income families—their health insurance premiums—and shift the weight to wealthier Americans by raising their taxes."[13] This is naïve. Public financing is necessary for pharmaceutical and other health care corporations to charge outrageous prices for goods and services while still getting paid.[17] Medicare for all will enable these same corporations to impoverish the working poor and middle class with crushing tax burdens so as to pay an ever increasing price for an ever decreasing quality of monopoly health care. Medicare for all would essentially convert every health care corporation into a cost plus rent seeking defense contractor.

The financial burdens of health care may be already taking a toll on working people. The CDC recently released data showing that life expectancy declined in the United States for the last two years with data (2015 and 2016).[18] This is very unusual for a developed country in the absence of war or some pandemic. These data also show that mortality rates increased for every age group between 15 and 64 while mortality decreased for every age group 65 and over. Subsidized health care does not seem to be working out well for those who have to pay the subsidies. While the causes for decreased life expectancy in developed countries is most likely multi-factorial, subsidized health care leads to fewer jobs available as manufacturers move to countries without health care taxes. For those who are fortunate to find jobs, subsidized health care taxes away a greater percentage of stagnant wages leaving less available for individual choices.

The ACA started with a promise—health insurance premiums will cost less—that could not possibly be kept. As the advocates of government subsidized health care forget the failings of ACA and

Universal Health Care

set their sights on Universal Coverage, we should be mindful that these promises of affordability will not be kept either.

Notes

1. 7 Key Promises Obamacare Broke. 2017, at http://www.dailywire.com/news/14725/7-key-promises-obamacare-broke-aaron-bandler

2. Lie of the Year: "If you like your health care plan, you can keep it." 2013, at http://www.politifact.com/truth-o-meter/article/2013/dec/12/lie-year-if-you-like-your-health-care-plan-keep-it/

3. Berdine, Gilbert. "Supply and Demand: Government Interference with the Unhampered Market in U.S. Health Care." The Southwest Respiratory and Critical Care Chronicles [Online], 2.7 (2014): 21-24. Web. 10 Jan. 2018.

4. No, Obamacare Hasn't Jacked Up Your Company's Insurance Rates. 2017, at https://www.forbes.com/sites/robbmandelbaum/2017/02/24/no-obamacare-hasnt-jacked-up-your-companys-insurance-rates/#5bfa5493a016

5. Yes, It Was the "Affordable" Care Act That Increased Premiums. 2017, https://www.forbes.com/sites/theapothecary/2017/03/22/yes-it-was-the-affordable-care-act-that-increased-premiums/#7b06f3e011d2

6. Ballotpedia. 2017, at https://ballotpedia.org/Scott_Rasmussen%27s_Number_of_the_Day_for_August_9_2017

7. CMS.gov Centers for Medicare and Medicaid Services. 2016, at https://www.cms.gov/Research-Statistics-Data-and-Systems/Statistics-Trends-and-Reports/NationalHealthExpendData/NationalHealthAccountsHistorical.html

8. One-third of US could see only one Obamacare option as insurers pull out. 2016, https://www.washingtontimes.com/news/2016/aug/29/aetna-unitedhealth-pulling-out-of-obamacare-leavin/

9. No, Obamacare Isn't in a "Death Spiral." 2017, at https://www.nytimes.com/2017/03/15/upshot/obamacare-isnt-in-a-death-spiral-its-replacement-probably-wont-be-either.html

10. How the Senate bill could send the health insurance market into a death spiral. 2017, at https://www.washingtonpost.com/news/wonk/wp/2017/06/23/republicans-say-the-health-insurance-market-is-in-a-death-spiral-their-bill-could-make-it-really-happen/

11. Trump to Scrap Critical Health Care Subsidies, Hitting Obamacare Again. 2017, at https://www.nytimes.com/2017/10/12/us/politics/trump-obamacare-executive-order-health-insurance.html

12. Aaron, H. Which Road to Universal Coverage?. *N Engl J Med* 2017 Dec 17:377(23):2207–09. http://www.nejm.org/doi/pdf/10.1056/NEJMp1713346

13. Morone, J. How to Think about "Medicare for All." *N Engl J Med* 2017 Dec 17:377(23):2209–11 http://www.nejm.org/doi/pdf/10.1056/NEJMp1713510

14. How the US sent $12bn in cash to Iraq. And watched it vanish. 2007, at https://www.theguardian.com/world/2007/feb/08/usa.iraq

15. "Vets continue to die": Phoenix hospital at center of VA scandal ranked among nation's worst. 2017, at http://www.foxnews.com/us/2017/02/09/vets-continue-to-die-phoenix-hospital-at-center-va-scandal-ranked-among-nations-worst.html

16. CMS.gov Centers for Medicare and Medicaid Services. 2017, at https://www.cms.gov/Research-Statistics-Data-and-Systems/Statistics-Trends-and-Reports/ReportsTrustFunds/Downloads/TR2017.pdf
17. Data Brief 293 Tables: Mortality in the United States. 2016 at https://www.cdc.gov/nchs/data/databriefs/db293_table.pdf#1
18. Why Some Pharmaceuticals Are So Expensive. 2017, at https://mises.org/blog/why-some-pharmaceuticals-are-so-expensive

14

Comparing US Health Costs to Other Countries

Aaron Hankin

Aaron Hankin has more than ten years of experience in the financial markets as a trader. In 2016, he changed careers to financial journalism. He has written for Investopedia and Dow Jones MarketWatch, and holds a master's degree in journalism from New York University.

As the United States continues to argue about universal health care and its costs and challenges, Aaron Hankin presents a look at health care insurance and services in other parts of the world in the following viewpoint. In particular, the author points out that medical care is significantly more expensive in the US when comparing similar medical care and procedures among several countries.

In another chapter of the ongoing debate over health care in the US, the International Federation of Health Plans Comparative Price Report takes a look at healthcare products and services around the world. The most recent survey (from 2015) looked at seven countries: the United States, the United Kingdom, Switzerland, Australia, New Zealand, South Africa and Spain. Results showed that not only were US healthcare costs elevated compared to the other countries in the survey, but there is also a

"How US Healthcare Costs Compare to Other Countries," by Aaron Hankin, Investopedia, a part of Dotdash Publishing Family, October 29, 2018. Reprinted by permission.

significant difference in what people pay in the US for the same drug or medical procedure.

Tom Sackville, chief executive of the IFHP, said many people believe, incorrectly, that Americans spend more time in a hospital and more time visiting the doctor or having procedures, which is what drives up prices. "That's not the case. It appears it's quite an efficient system—they don't overuse it," Sackville said. "But each time they have an item, an episode of care, it costs two or three or five times more than it should, by international standards."

In its study, the Federation wanted to prove that the issue is unit costs, not about utilization as many people think. Prices in the US are on a like-for-like basis higher than their counterparts in other countries.

The data for the US were extracted from more than 370 million medical claims and more than 170 million pharmacy claims, which the Federation says reflect prices negotiated and paid to health care providers. Prices from the six other countries were obtained from the private sector provided by one health plan in each nation. When comparing procedures across the seven countries, the Federation ensured that the entire process was "like-for-like, across international boundaries," Sackville said. For example, when comparing the price for a standard MRI scan, the data came from procedures where identical types of machines were used with equal staffing resources per procedure.

Comparing Price Differences

Not only did the Federation conclude that the average price in the US is far higher than anywhere else, but it also found a wide disparity in the prices paid within the US. Sackville called the considerable variation in cost "completely unwarranted for any clinical reason."

For example, the average cost in the US for an MRI scan was $1,119, compared to $811 in New Zealand, $215 in Australia and $181 in Spain. However, data showed that the 95th percentile in the price of this procedure in the US was $3,031, meaning some people are paying nearly $3,000 more for a standard MRI scan in the US than the average person in Australia and Spain.

Or take a standard hip-replacement procedure. The average cost in the US is $29,067, which is $10,000 more than the next highest-cost country, Australia. However, the data show that the 95th percentile cost in the US reaches $57,225, $50,000 more than the average price in South Africa and $42,000 more than in New Zealand. The results for knee replacements are much the same. Sackville added that the study suggests that the more expensive procedures are no better than the average or cheap ones.

The researchers also observed the trend in prescription drugs. Avastin, prescribed as a treatment for certain types of cancer, has an average price of $3,930 in the US. Switzerland is the second most expensive at $1,752. However, the data found that the 95th percentile in the US paid up to $8,831. Avastin costs $470 in the UK. Similar trends were observed in Truvada (a treatment for HIV/AIDS), Harvoni (hepatitis C), Humira (rheumatoid arthritis) and Xarelto (blood clot prevention). One outlier was OxyContin, a general painkiller that is the most expensive in the UK at $590 per prescription, with the US finishing second in cost at an average of $265. (Note: the prices are based on a 4-week to one month supply)

Why the US Costs So Much

So why are medical costs considerably more expensive in the US.?

According to the researchers, the idea that the US has a higher cost of living that drives up healthcare costs is a common fallacy. Numbeo is a crowd-sourced global database that bi-annually ranks countries by their cost of living. Its 2018 mid-year ranking has the United States at 21st, two places ahead of the UK. Switzerland is first, New Zealand 17th, Australia 15th, Spain 34th, and South Africa at 70th. So, the overall cost of living seems an unlikely candidate for why healthcare in the US is so expensive.

A lack of competition appears to be closer to the root of the problem, and hospital mergers are one development that has stifled competition. In March 2016, Kellogg School of Management at

Northwestern University wrote a paper titled "The Price Effects of Cross-Market Hospital Mergers" in which researchers explored the cost of health care after the consolidation of hospitals in the same geographic market. The report concluded that merged hospitals in similar geographic regions are likely to have had similar customers and insurers, which reduces competition. "The results suggest that cross-market, within-state hospital mergers appear to increase hospital systems' leverage when bargaining with insurers," the report said.

"We find that hospitals gaining system members in-state (but not in the same geographic market) experience price increases of 6-10 percent relative to control hospitals, while hospitals gaining system members out-of-state show no statistically significant changes in price."

This is a sentiment shared by Tom Sackville, who says, "When there's anti-competitive behavior going on like consolidation of whole hospitals, which ends up driving prices up. No one does anything about it." Sackville added, "this may be not unconnected to the fact that all these people have a lot of lobbyists working in Washington and they are making themselves very amenable to local politicians."

In addition to the consolidation in hospitals, anti-competitive pricing behavior has been facilitated by mergers of health insurance companies. In mid-July 2016, the US antitrust officials sought to block two major acquisitions in the health insurance sector for fear it would reduce competition and drive up prices.

The Bottom Line

Whether it is the consolidation of hospitals and other health services or anti-competitive pricing behavior, healthcare costs in the US are rising at an alarming rate, a rate that far surpasses wage inflation.

Health Affairs has projected that between 2015 and 2025 spending on health care will grow at 5.8% per year. By 2025, it will make up 20.1% of US GDP. This is a disturbing figure that is trending in the wrong direction.

"There is no reason why identical procedures and products should vary in price so much across countries: it illustrates the damaging effects of an inadequately regulated healthcare market," Sackville said.

15

A Free-Market Solution to Health Care Reform

Kent Holtorf

Dr. Kent Holtorf is an endocrinologist and the founder of the Holtorf Medical Group, and a board examiner for the American Board of Anti-Aging Medicine. He received his doctorate in medicine from St. Louis University with residency training at UCLA. He was the founding medical director and developed the protocols for Fibromyalgia and Fatigue Centers and other medical centers across the country.

In the following viewpoint, Kent Holtorf states that the only way to reform the Affordable Care Act and put in place a universal health care system for the United States is by using the free-market system to really address the underlying problems with health care in this country and to lower health care costs. This is the only way to build affordable health care for every US citizen, he argues.

Repealing and replacing the Affordable Care Act is on indefinite life support. The political consensus was that President Trump needed to pass health care reform to be able to move forward with his legislative agenda. While this may be true, the passing of any repeal and replacement bill without fundamental reforms has little chance of long-term success, likely defining Trump's presidency as a failure no matter how successful he is in other areas. The

"Health Care Reform: A Free-Market Solution Works in Other Countries," by Kent Holtorf, KevinMD, LLC, September 13, 2017. Reprinted by permission.

proposed replacement bill, the American Health care Act (AHA), offered no major changes to the fundamentals of one of the most bureaucratic, inefficient, rationed and corrupt health care delivery systems in the world.

The US spends over $10,000 per capita on health care, more than twice the average of other developed countries, though consistently ranking among the least efficient in the world. Much of the excess cost is a consequence of trying to use an insurance model for routine care, which eliminates competition and consumer-driven cost controls. The US far exceeds any nation in expenditures for insurance administration, where the essential means of cost control is denial of service and rationing of care via ever increasing complex treatment approval systems, resulting in spiraling costs. Insurance is designed to provide coverage for medical emergencies, not routine care. Insurance has never worked in any industry as a method of providing services that are used on a routine basis.

Both physicians and patients, Republicans and Democrats alike, agree that increased access to health care and consumer choice are two of the most important aspects of health care reform. Many feel, however, that these are essentially mutually exclusive goals—feeling that increasing patient access to care means becoming a more socialized system while increasing consumer choice requires a free-market system, sacrificing patient access. Fortunately, these are not mutually exclusive goals.

The misconception that the American health care system is a free market system and the European systems are socialized because they provide universal coverage are complete fallacies. The American health care system has less consumer choice and other free market principles than most every industrialized nation even though they are often referred to as socialized medicine. US government (taxpayer) funded health care spending is the highest of any country in the amount spent per capita, as a percent of GDP and as the percent paid by government compared to private payments. At 65 percent, it exceeds any nation, including those

A Free-Market Solution to Health Care Reform

with universal health care programs such as the United Kingdom, Sweden, Canada and France.

Countries vary dramatically in the degree of regulation, central control, cost sharing and the function of private insurance. However, overall trends from the different health care delivery systems demonstrate that:

- The more heavily weighted the system is toward government control, the more likely the patients face significant restrictions on physician choice, long wait times, rationed care and other obstacles.
- Having health insurance does not necessarily mean increased access to care, but instead rationed care with long wait times for treatment or services.
- The more the health care system incorporates free-market mechanisms, such as competition, cost sharing (copays), transparency, consistent pricing for all goods and services, consumer choice with an incentive and ability to discern price and value of goods and services and rejection of government control, the more effective the health care system.

The US system is very similar to the systems used in France and Switzerland, with both having one underlying significant difference from the US—more free-market mechanisms to maintain costs, including consumer choice, price transparency, fewer regulations and consistent cost-sharing (copays of 10 to 40 percent) to discourage overuse of services. The Swiss system has been considered an ideal model of socialized medicine, but there are no government run insurance plans and no public options. It is based on a managed competition model, which is essentially the basis of the US system, with a few differences. One such difference is the requirement for everyone to purchase catastrophic insurance (there is no employer contribution), but government subsidies are offered to individuals to buy coverage from private insurers.

Additionally, most Swiss purchase a health savings account, giving the Swiss more consumer control than could ever be

Universal Health Care

imagined in the US. Due to these consumer controls of health care purchasing and consistent cost-sharing, they pay 40 percent less for a comparable level of health care to the US, with consumers generally being responsible for 20 percent of the cost. A review of the Swiss health care system published in *JAMA* concluded, "Cost control may be attributed to the Swiss consumer's significant role in health care payments and the resulting cost transparency."

Singapore is arguably the best health care system, ranked sixth in the world in the WHO Quality of Care and second only to Hong Kong in efficiency while paying about one-fifth of what Americans pay for health care. Often referred to as a socialized health care system because everyone is required to purchase a Health Savings Account (HSA), it is also the most free-market oriented system in the world, as patients are aware of costs and can use their HSA money to shop around for the best value for their health.

Unlike the US system, the Singapore health care system promotes individual responsibility with significant incentives for patients to make health care choices that provide value while allowing market forces to improve service, increase efficiency and foster the development of patient options. Patients then purchase a high deductible insurance plan with their HSA money for significant unforeseen medical problems. The key to success of the system is the widespread use of HSAs, where consumers have ultimate control when combined with price transparency. In this country, most believe that free market competition entails having multiple insurance companies to choose from, which completely misses the entire concept of free market and will not have a significant lasting impact on health care costs.

The model that works in other countries, utilizing HSAs for routine care combined with a high deductible plan for emergency coverage, would work in the US but would require market reform. Regulations would be needed that allow consumer choice, including price transparency, and prevent the grossly inflated arbitrary pricing of hospitals, laboratories and drug companies that are different depending on who is buying. Thus, requirements that those supplying the product or service post their prices and cannot charge different amounts to consumers based on insurance coverage or carrier will be needed.

In my communications with members of Congress, it seems clear that there is no incentive to reform health care and an unwillingness to take on powerful health care lobbies. One congressperson's office responded with, "Long story short, we are screwed regardless of what legislation is passed …" This sentiment seems to be common, in that they don't believe or see a way to successfully reform health care or are unwilling to make the necessary reforms. If Congress is willing to put the health care of the American public above their concerns about making significant change to the current system, which can be risky when seeking re-election, dramatic improvement in the health care system is possible.

A free-market system is shown to be the only reasonable method of reform that addresses the true underlying problems of the US health care system and effectively lowers health care costs, allowing for universal insurance coverage for most everyone so any reasonable person—doctor, patient, Republican or Democrat—could support.

16

The Case for a Two-Tier Health System

Jonathan Gruber

Jonathan Gruber, PhD, is a professor of economics at the Massachusetts Institute of Technology and the director of the Health Care Program at the National Bureau of Economic Research. Dr. Gruber's research focuses on the areas of public finance and health economics. He has written more than 150 published research articles and is the associate editor of the Journal of Public Economics *and the* Journal of Health Economics.

Politicians agree on the need for health care reform, but they disagree as to the best way to create a program and pay for it. While many countries have a single-payer system, where the government gives its citizens a uniform package of health coverage, the author of this viewpoint argues that this system won't work in the US. He argues that a two-tiered insurance system is the only feasible option. This viewpoint was written before the Affordable Care Act was signed into law.

While Democrats (and some Republicans) have long agreed on fundamental health reform centered on universal insurance coverage, that is where the agreement ends. There are a wide variety of reform models, and a number of different ways to get to universal coverage. Many argue that the only logical approach to such reform is a single-payer system, as in Canada,

"The Case for a Two-Tier Health System," by Jonathan Gruber, Massachusetts Institute of Technology, Winter 2009. Reprinted by permission.

The Case for a Two-Tier Health System

where one monopoly government insurer provides coverage for the entire population. Every resident of Canada is entitled to a uniform package of insurance benefits with limited patient cost-sharing. This approach has a number of major efficiency advantages, including lower administrative costs and maximum bargaining power for the insurer (the government) in negotiations with providers, which keep medical costs much lower than in the United States. It also may lead to much more equalized outcomes of the health care system than does a piecemeal system of insurance.

At the same time, such an approach is highly unlikely to succeed in the United States for two reasons. First, it would displace the majority of insured Americans who are largely satisfied with the health insurance they receive from their employers. Second, it would require nationalizing an industry, private health insurance, with more than $500 billion in revenues per year. These barriers are not likely to be overcome in the foreseeable future.

For this reason, policymakers have been turning to a new model that I label "incremental universalism": moving to universal health insurance coverage by building on the existing system of (largely employer-based) private health insurance and filling in the cracks through which the uninsured are likely to fall. The example most commonly used to illustrate this model is the ambitious health reform that began in late 2006 in the state of Massachusetts. This plan had several key features: heavily subsidized insurance for low-income residents that is very comprehensive (with limited copayments and no deductibles); market reform for other residents so that everyone else in the uninsured and small-group insurance markets purchase through a pooled market where prices cannot vary by health (and only in a limited way by age); and an individual mandate that imposes large fines on residents who do not have health insurance coverage unless they meet a set of narrow exemption guidelines (exempting about 15 percent of the uninsured on income grounds).

This plan leaves intact the employer-based system for firms with more than 50 employees. Most of the insurance coverage in the state continues to be provided via this employer-based model. It is perhaps for this reason that the plan was able to pass.

Thus far, the plan has been quite successful, with the most recent estimate reporting an uninsurance rate of only 2.6 percent, by far the lowest in the nation and perhaps as close to universal coverage as is feasible in the United States. Costs have been high, but in line with projections of about $1 billion for fiscal year 2009. This implies a cost of about $2,000 per newly insured person, which is very low by the standard of other options for increasing health insurance coverage.

Universal Coverage and Inequality

Single-payer and "incremental universalism" are just two examples of models that can lead the United States to universal health insurance coverage. Yet these two models, as well as other alternatives, can have very different implications for the inequality of health outcomes in our society. Indeed, the primary concern for advocates of universal coverage should be this level of inequality. For the most advantaged members of society today, both health care and health outcomes are excellent; for example, the white infant mortality rate in the United States is comparable to rates in other developed nations. The fundamental problem with the US health system, and the one reflected in our poor international comparisons, is the terrible outcomes of the most disadvantaged members of society: the black infant mortality rate in the United States is twice the white rate, and is higher than the rates in either Barbados or Malaysia.

In this essay, I step back to discuss the determinants of health inequality and how it plays into the structure of universal coverage. Health status inequality in any nation will be the product of several factors. The first, and most important, is inequality in non-medical factors. This ranges from nutrition to exercise to smoking to safety, and is largely beyond the influence of the medical system. These non-medical sources of inequality should be the primary focus of any campaign to reduce health disparities. Perhaps the single best source of improvement in the health of Americans over the past 50 years has been the reduction in cigarette smoking, and a serious gun control policy might do as much or more for the health of Americans as any expansion of insurance coverage. Although these issues around non-medical inequality are both important and fascinating, they are beyond the purview of this article.

Of the remaining health inequality that is amenable to medical intervention, the three factors that matter are uniformity of *coverage*, uniformity of *access*, and uniformity of *quality*. By uniformity of coverage, I mean uniformity in the comprehensiveness with which medical care is covered by insurance, and the costs that individuals have to pay out of pocket to use that care. By uniformity of access I mean uniformity in the availability of nearby physicians and hospital care. And by uniformity of quality I mean uniformity in the skill level of the providers to which individuals have access.

In practice, it is infeasible to achieve perfect uniformity along all three of these dimensions. Consider uniformity of access. Given the enormous differences in population density in countries such as the United States, it would be incredibly inefficient to guarantee every citizen a physician within 5 miles of his or her home, or even perhaps within 25 miles.

Minimum Standards

So the question becomes: What should developed nations strive for as standards in these areas? I believe that the right approach is to move toward an explicit two-tier medical system, whereby society sets minimum standards in each of these areas, but then allows individuals to buy higher coverage, access, or quality using their own resources. In fact, such is the approach used by most single-payer nations that have an explicit national health program: They allow individuals to buy extra insurance or care using their own funds.

But this is not the approach currently used in the United States. There are no explicit standards for what constitutes minimum acceptable standards for coverage, access, and quality. As a result, we have many individuals falling below any reasonable acceptable minimum in each category, while most others end up subsidized to levels well above such minima. This extremely unequal patchwork system must be reformed. At the same time, it is fiscally impossible to bring every American up to the highest standard of coverage, access, and quality. Therefore, the question becomes: What is an acceptable minimum standard that can form the basis for a two-tier system?

The best example of this issue is the generosity of insurance coverage. Forty-seven million Americans have no health insurance coverage, and that figure is only going to grow due to recent economic hardships. Yet the vast majority of the remaining Americans actually have too much insurance coverage, in that they are induced to use medical care beyond the point where it is cost effective. This is clear from the famous RAND Health Insurance Experiment of the 1970s. In this experiment, individuals were randomly assigned to plans with more or less individual cost-sharing; some received health care for free, while others had to pay 95 percent of the costs up to an out-of-pocket limit that was roughly $5,000 in today's dollars. As one might expect, the individuals who were less comprehensively covered used less health care; for example, those for whom health care was free used 50 percent more care than those who had to pay 95 percent of the costs. What was more surprising was that, on average, they were in no worse health. That is, the marginal health care utilization that was induced by more generous insurance coverage did not improve health.

Why do individuals typically have insurance coverage that covers care that does not seem to improve health? There are a variety of reasons, but one is that the government subsidizes them to do so. Individuals who receive their health insurance through their employers pay taxes on their wages but not on the value of their health insurance. This tax subsidy, which amounts to foregone revenues to the government of over $250 billion/year (making it the third largest health care program in the United States), induces individuals to purchase excessively generous insurance coverage.

Given these facts, how should health insurance coverage be reformed to increase equality in a fiscally responsible manner? First and foremost, all citizens must be guaranteed some form of insurance coverage. But that base level should be no more generous than is necessary to produce health efficiently. This would be achieved by a plan that made individuals pay their up-front costs of health care, but with an out-of-pocket maximum that is income-related so no family is bankrupted by their health care needs.

At the same time, the government should allow individuals who wish to purchase more generous coverage to do so. Without this "escape mechanism," there will be enormous pressure to continually ratchet upward the generosity of the base level to meet the needs of higher-income individuals who prefer, and can afford, to be over-insured. However, a key change must be to end government subsidies to insurance coverage that are above that base level: If higher-income individuals want to buy more generous coverage, they should be allowed to, but not with government-subsidized dollars. Such a two-tier system can then ensure that all have cost-effective insurance coverage, while also reducing government expenditures on health care.

Another example of an explicit two-tier approach is with respect to quality of care. As researchers at Dartmouth and elsewhere have emphasized, there are enormous discrepancies in the quality of care that is delivered around the United States. For example, sensible preventive measures, such as the use of beta blockers after a heart attack, are ignored by a sizeable share of primary care doctors and specialists around the nation.

A clear move toward equality in health would be to both penalize poor-quality care and reward high-quality care through reimbursement incentives. Once again, society must address the key question of a minimum level of quality that it is willing to accept for all citizens. Having defined that, both public and private insurers need to pay providers only if they meet those minimum standards. Such "pay for performance" measures are slowly being adopted in the United States, but in a haphazard way. Once again, however, insurance plans may adopt higher standards for quality and charge more as a result. Individuals who want to pay more for such plans should not be restricted from doing so, but should not be subsidized in any way for those purchases.

In summary, the United States could move to a health care system that is much more equal—but it is impossible, and impractical, to demand perfect equality of health outcomes, or even of health insurance inputs. Rather than hold out for perfect equality, the focus of action should be in two areas. The first is defining a universally accepted minimum, then ensuring that all citizens receive that minimum, be it with respect to health insurance generosity, quality of care, or other features. The second is to allow individuals to purchase above that minimum—but not to subsidize such purchases through the government. Any public resources devoted to this problem should be devoted to financing an acceptable minimum, not to promoting choices beyond that level.

Organizations to Contact

The editors have compiled the following list of organizations concerned with the issues debated in this book. The descriptions are derived from materials provided by the organizations. All have publications or information available for interested readers. The list was compiled on the date of publication of the present volume; the information provided here may change. Be aware that many organizations take several weeks or longer to respond to inquiries, so allow as much time as possible.

American Medical Association
AMA Plaza
330 N. Wabash Avenue, Suite 39300
Chicago, IL 60611-5885
(800) 621-8335
website: www.ama-assn.org

The American Medical Association is the largest association of physicians and medical students in the United States. The AMA's mission is "to promote the art and science of medicine and the betterment of public health." It works with physicians, practices, and students and promotes medical research and ethics.

The American Medical Student Association (AMSA)
45610 Woodland Road #300
Sterling, VA 20166
(703) 620-6600
email: amsa@amsa.org
website: www.amsa.org

AMSA is a student-governed, national organization committed to representing the concerns of physicians-in-training. AMSA members are medical students, premedical students, interns, residents, and practicing physicians. AMSA is committed to improving medical training and the nation's health. One of its campaigns is to advocate for universal health care for all.

Families USA
1225 New York Avenue NW
Suite 800
Washington, DC 20005
(202) 628-3030
email: info@familiesusa.org
website: https://familiesusa.org

Families USA is a leading national voice for health care consumers and works to achieve high-quality, affordable health care and improved health for all. It uses public policy analysis, advocacy, and collaboration with partners to promote a patient- and community-centered health system.

Healthcare – Now!
9A Hamilton Place
Boston, MA 02108
(215) 732-2131
email: info@healthcare-now.org
website: www.healthcare-now.org

Healthcare–Now is an advocacy group building a social movement to achieve a national single-payer health care system through education and outreach. It brings together the voices of patients struggling with the health care system, educates activists, and mobilizes its network through collective action.

Kaiser Family Foundation
1330 G Street NW
Washington, DC 20005
(202) 347-5270
email via website
website: www.kff.org

The Kaiser Family Foundation is an American nonprofit organization that focuses on major health care issues facing the nation, as well as the US role in global health policy.

National Institutes of Health (NIH)
US Department of Health and Human Services
9000 Rockville Pike
Bethesda, MD 20892
(301) 496-4000
website: www.nih.gov

The National Institutes of Health is the United States' medical research agency. It conducts research and makes discoveries to improve health and save lives. The NIH is made up of 27 different components called Institutes and Centers. Each has its own specific research agenda, often focusing on particular diseases or body systems.

Physicians for a National Health Program (PNHP)
29 E. Madison Street, Suite 1412
Chicago, IL 60602
(312) 782-6006
email: info@pnhp.org
website: https://pnhp.org

PNHP's mission is to advocate for universal, comprehensive single-payer national health insurance. It educates physicians, other health workers, and the general public on the need for a comprehensive, high-quality, publicly funded health care program, equitably accessible to all residents of the United States.

Universal Health Care Action Network (UHCAN)
2800 Euclid Avenue, Suite 520
Cleveland, OH 44115
(866) 981-5007
email: uhcan@uhcan.org
website: https://uhcan.org

UHCAN is a health care advocacy group working for universal health care and health care justice for everyone. It builds unity among groups working for universal health care, connects and supports state and local health care justice groups and connects them to national organizations working for health care justice, and creates relationships between the health care justice movement and other social and economic justice movements.

US Centers for Medicare & Medicaid Services (CMS)
7500 Security Boulevard
Baltimore, MD 21244
(877) 267-2323
email via website
website: www.cms.gov

CMS is part of the US Department of Health and Human Services. It helps patients with Medicaid, Medicare, and the Health Insurance Exchanges to work with their doctors and make health care decisions that are best for them. It provides information about quality and costs to help patients be active health care consumers, and supports innovative approaches to improving quality, accessibility, and affordability.

World Health Organization (WHO)
WHO Headquarters in Geneva
Avenue Appia 20
1202 Geneva, Switzerland
email via website
website: www.who.int

WHO works worldwide to promote health, keep the world safe, and serve the vulnerable. Its goal is to ensure that a billion more people have universal health coverage, to protect a billion more people from health emergencies, and provide a further billion people with better health and well-being.

Bibliography

Books

Stuart Altman and David Shactman, *Power, Politics, and Universal Health Care: The Inside Story of a Century-Long Battle.* Amherst, NY: Prometheus Books, 2011.

Steven Brill, *America's Bitter Pill: Money, Politics, Backroom Deals, and the Fight to Fix Our Broken Healthcare System.* New York, NY: Random House, 2015.

John C. Burnham, *Health Care in America: A History.* Baltimore, MD: Johns Hopkins University Press, 2015.

Andrea Louise Campbell, *Trapped in America's Safety Net: One Family's Struggle.* Chicago, IL: University of Chicago Press, 2014.

Ezekiel J. Emanuel, *Reinventing American Health Care: How the Affordable Care Act Will Improve Our Terribly Complex, Blatantly Unjust, Outrageously Expensive, Grossly Inefficient, Error Prone System.* New York, NY: Public Affairs Books, 2015.

Susan Dudley Gold, *Health Care Reform Act.* New York, NY: Cavendish Square, 2011.

Kristina Lyn Heitkamp, *Universal Health Care.* New York, NY: Greenhaven Publishing, 2018.

David A. Hyman, *Overcharged: Why Americans Pay Too Much for Health Care.* Washington, DC: Cato Institute Press, 2018.

Marty Makary, *The Price We Pay: What Broke American Health Care—and How to Fix It.* New York, NY: Bloomsbury Press, 2019.

Corinne J. Naden and Erin L. McCoy, *Health Care: Universal Right or Personal Responsibility?* New York, NY: Cavendish Square, 2019.

Sally C. Pipes, *The False Promise of Single-Payer Health Care.* New York, NY: Encounter Books, 2018.

T. R. Reid, *The Healing of America: A Global Quest for Better, Cheaper, and Fairer Health Care.* New York, NY: Penguin, 2009.

Paul Starr, *Remedy and Reaction: The Peculiar American Struggle over Health Care Reform,* revised edition. New Haven, CT: Yale University Press, 2013.

Jeffrey L. Sturchio, et al., *The Road to Universal Health Coverage: Innovation, Equity, and the New Health Economy.* Baltimore, MD: Johns Hopkins University Press, 2019.

William G. Weissert and Carol S. Weissert, *Governing Health: The Politics of Health Policy.* Baltimore, MD: Johns Hopkins University Press, 2012.

Periodicals and Internet Sources

Kimberly Amadeo, "Why America Is the Only Rich Country Without Universal Health Care." The Balance, April 25, 2019. https://www.thebalance.com/universal-health-care-4156211.

"The Best Health Care System in the World: Which One Would You Pick?" *New York Times,* September 18, 2017. https://www.nytimes.com/interactive/2017/09/18/upshot/best-health-care-system-country-bracket.html.

Linda J. Blumberg and John Holahan, "The Pros and Cons of Single-Payer Health Plans." Urban Institute, March 2019. https://www.urban.org/sites/default/files/publication/99918/pros_and_cons_of_a_single-payer_plan.pdf.

Matt Bruenig, "Universal Health Care Might Cost You Less Than You Think." *New York Times,* April 29, 2019. https://www.nytimes.com/2019/04/29/opinion/medicare-for-all-cost.html.

Bibliography

Health Research Funding, "Universal Healthcare Pros and Cons." Accessed April 29, 2019. https://healthresearchfunding.org/universal-healthcare-pros-cons.

Kaiser Family Foundation, "Different Takes: Pros and Cons of 'Medicare for All'; Pinpoint Smaller Tweaks That Make a Big Cost Difference." August 28, 2018. https://khn.org/morning-breakout/different-takes-pros-and-cons-of-medicare-for-all-pinpoint-smaller-tweaks-that-make-a-big-cost-difference.

Joe Messerli, "Should the Government Provide Free Universal Health Care for All Americans?" Balanced Politics. Accessed April 29, 2019. https://www.balancedpolitics.org/universal_health_care.htm.

Mark Pauly and Robert Field, "Could Universal Health Care Work in the US?" Knowledge @ Wharton, February 22, 2019. https://knowledge.wharton.upenn.edu/article/could-universal-health-care-work-in-the-u-s/.

Sintia Radu, "Countries with the Most Well-Developed Public Health Care Systems." *U.S. News and World Report*, February 4, 2019. https://www.usnews.com/news/best-countries/slideshows/countries-with-the-most-well-developed-public-health-care-system.

Amartya Sen, "Universal Health Care: The Affordable Dream." *Harvard Public Health Review*. http://harvardpublichealthreview.org/universal-health-care-the-affordable-dream.

United Nations, "The Universal Declaration of Human Rights." United Nations, 1948. https://www.un.org/en/universal-declaration-human-rights/.

United Nations/World Health Organization, "The Right to Health." Fact Sheet #31. United Nations. Accessed April 29, 2019. https://www.ohchr.org/documents/publications/factsheet31.pdf.

World Health Organization, "Questions and Answers on Universal Health Coverage." Accessed April 29, 2019. https://www.who.int/healthsystems/topics/financing/uhc_qa/en.

World Health Organization, "What Is Health Financing for Universal Coverage?" Accessed April 29, 2019. https://www.who.int/health_financing/universal_coverage_definition/en.

Index

A

Affordable Care Act (ACA)/
  Obamacare, 8–9, 18, 19,
  20, 21, 35, 36, 40, 41, 46,
  63, 65–67, 77, 78, 85,
  91–99, 105
Amadeo, Kimberly, 52–56
American Health Care Act,
  63, 65–67, 106
American Medical
  Association, and role
  in creating insurance
  company model, 36–38, 79
Austin, Daniel A., 54
Australia, health care costs,
  100, 101, 102

B

bankruptcy, medical, 52–56, 78
Berdine, Gilbert, 91–99
Bismarck, Otto von, 29
Blahous, Charles, 72
Braithwaite, Kisha, 11–17
Brazil, health care in, 28

C

Canada, health care in, 7–8, 9,
  69, 72, 73, 84, 89, 90, 107,
  110–111
Center for Health and
  Economy, 72
Centers for Disease Control
  (CDC), 84, 97
Centers for Medicare and
  Medicaid Services (CMS),
  42, 43
Chapin, Christy Ford, 35–41
Children's Health Insurance
  Program, 43, 69, 70
Chile, health care in, 28
Clinton, Bill, 72, 80
Clinton, Hillary, 40, 79
Cohen, Wilbur, 81
Conyers, John, 70
copays, 49, 51, 59, 71, 107, 111

D

Debt.org, 54
deductibles, 40, 48, 49, 51, 55,
  56, 78, 89, 108, 111
Democratic Party/Democrats,
  9, 14, 29, 68, 77–79, 80, 81,
  106, 109, 110
Dolan, Ed, 61–67

E

Eisenhower, Dwight, 39
Ellison, Keith, 70
emergency room use vs.
  primary care, 57–60
employer-sponsored insurance,
  8, 63, 66, 69, 90, 92, 111, 114

Expanded and Improved Medicare for All Act, 70–71, 80

F

Federal Insurance Contributions Act, 50
France, health care in, 107
Frank, Ategeka, 22–25
free-market solution to health care reform, 105–109

G

Gaffney, Adam, 77–82
Galan, Nicole, 42–51
Galles, Gary M., 18–21
Grande, David, 60
Greer, Scott L., 26–34
Gross, Tal, 53
Gruber, Jonathan, 110–116

H

Hankin, Aaron, 100–104
Health Affairs, 57, 58, 103
health, as human right, 7, 11–17
health care costs, US, vs. other countries, 14, 67, 84, 100–104, 106, 108
health inequality, 112–113, 115–116
health insurance
  employer-based, 8, 63, 66, 69, 90, 92, 111, 114

history of insurance company model, 36–40
how it works, 18–21
Holtorf, Kent, 105–109
Hong Kong, health care in, 108

I

incremental universalism, 111, 112
Indian Health Services, 73
individual mandate, 93–95, 111
insurance companies, 21, 35–41, 49, 51, 55, 64-65, 79, 81, 93, 94, 103, 108
International Federation of Health Plans, 100, 101

J

Japan, health insurance expansion in, 29
Johnson, Lyndon B., 42, 86

K

Kaiser Family Foundation, 54, 55, 64, 66
Kangovi, Shreya, 58, 59, 60

L

Latin America, health care in, 28
Lazarus, David, 18
life expectancy, US, 12, 97
Long, Judith, 60

Index

M

McCain, John, 14
Medicaid, 8, 9, 42–43, 58, 59, 61, 62, 69, 70, 71, 85, 88, 90, 93
  what it is, 43
  what services are covered, 43–44
  who is eligible for, 45–46, 50
  who pays for, 46–47
Medicare, 8, 18, 21, 39, 42–43, 54, 61, 62, 69, 70, 71, 72, 74, 78, 79, 80–81, 85, 88, 89–90, 91–92, 93, 95, 96, 97
  Medicare Part A, 47–48
  Medicare Part B, 48, 89
  Medicare Part C, 49
  Medicare Part D, 49, 89
  what it is, 47–50
  who is eligible for, 50
  who pays for, 50–51
Medicare for All, 21, 69, 70–71, 74, 78, 79, 80, 81, 95, 96, 97
Medicare for All Act, 69, 70–71, 72, 73, 74, 81
Medigap plans, 49
Méndez, Claudio A., 26–34
mental health/illness, 12, 15, 60
Mercadante, Kevin, 83–90
Mexico, health care in, 29

N

NerdWallet Health, 53, 54

New Zealand, health care costs, 100, 101, 102
Nixon, Richard, 80
Notowidigbo, Matthew, 53

O

Obama, Barack/Obama administration, 9, 14, 52, 53, 77–78, 79, 91, 93
Ocasio-Cortez, Alexandria, 79
Organisation for Economic Co-operation and Development, 84

P

Paulton, Meridian, 68–76
Physicians for a National Health Program, 80
pre-existing conditions, 20, 64, 65, 93–94, 92, 95
prepaid physician/doctor groups, 36–37, 40, 41

R

Reagan, Ronald, 80
refugees, 22, 23–25
Republican Party/Republicans, 14, 41, 61, 63, 66, 67, 78, 80, 94, 106, 109, 110
Robert Wood Johnson Foundation, 57–60
Ryan, Paul, 78

127

S

Sackville, Tom, 101–102, 103, 104
Sanders, Bernie, 69, 70–71, 72, 73, 79, 81
Self-Employment Contributions Act (SECA), 50
Singapore, health care in, 108
single-payer health care, 18, 21, 61–67, 68–76, 77–82, 83, 110, 112, 113
Social Security Act, 42
South Africa, health care costs, 100, 102
Spain, health care costs, 100, 101, 102
Sweden, health care in, 107
Switzerland, health care in, 100, 102, 107–108

T

Tax Policy Center, 62
Thorpe, Ken, 72
Truman, Harry, 37, 39, 79, 81
Trump, Donald/Trump administration, 9, 18, 41, 78, 94, 105
two-tier health system, 110–116

U

UHC2030, 22, 24–25
United Kingdom, health care in, 7–8, 9, 69, 72, 73, 100, 102, 107
United Nations, 7, 22
Universal Declaration of Human Rights, 7
universal health care
politics of, 9, 26–34, 77–82
as priority, 22–25
why it won't work in the US, 83–90
Universal Health Coverage Day, 22, 24–25
Urban Institute, 71, 72

V

Veterans Administration, 62, 73

W

Warren, Elizabeth, 53
World Health Organization, 7, 8, 11, 27, 108